I0639711

Silver Buckles

Lindy Larsen, Volume 1

Gayle Siebert

Published by Idyllbeck Opportunities, 2024.

SILVER BUCKLES

First edition. February 18, 2024.

ISBN: 978-1990180354

Written by Gayle Siebert.

Table of Contents

ONE

Calgary, Alberta, Canada

Sunday, July 18, 1976

"Yer hitched up 'n' loaded," Porky says. "That was bad luck in the steer rasslin' but you still got a couple rides this afternoon, ain't you?"

Scowling, the mud-splattered cowboy ignores the question and glowers across the parking lot at a young couple. Soft, unlined faces close, they stand partly sheltered by the empty bleachers, bodies pressed together, oblivious to the downpour.

Tossing his gloves into his rope can, he snaps the lid shut and clucks disdainfully. When he bends to unzip his chaps, rain collected in the wide brim of his stained hat spills down the front of his shirt. He pulls the batwings off and heaps them in the tack compartment of the Bondo-mottled trailer. Without looking up, he says, "Time to go."

He flips the rope can on edge and grips its handle with a swollen hand, wincing. Switching hands, he hoists it into the trailer with a clatter, then pulls a stretched-out Tensor bandage from a bin on the tack room door, pushes his sleeve up, and starts winding it in a figure eight around his already taped wrist.

"Got a burr under yer saddle? Over that buckle bunny 'n' Painless?"

"Hell no!" But he glowers at the young couple again before he turns his attention to the bin, comes up with the metal clips for the Tensor and sticks them on the bandage. Then he slams the compartment door, giving it a tug to make sure it's latched. Mud sucks at his boots as he hobbles around the rig, checking lights, latches, tires, before climbing into the driver's seat and slamming the door. "Wrecked my goddamn wrist again," he explains through the partly open window. "Got it taped up good'n tight but still can't git a good hold on nuthin'. Lookit how swole up it is, can barely git my glove on. Anyhow, Diamond don't like bein' wet 'n' cold no more'n I do. I'm takin' him home."

"You could put him in the barn here, go fer that reride 'n' still git into the standings for the championship," Porky points out, and spews a dark stream of Copenhagen spit. "Put the rein in yer left hand. The Cameron Larsen I grew up with had bigger balls'n that."

Larsen's eyes, crinkled with crow's feet but still a deep, unwavering blue, meet his friend's. His expression softens. "Goddamn you, Porky. You know one time I'd'a rode rain or shine. Hurtin' or not. Whether my horse fell or not. I'd of won, too. Lost my determination, I guess. Them was my glory days 'n' I gotta learn they're in my rear-view now. When a filly turns down steak with me fer a burger with Painless..." His gaze drifts off with his thoughts.

"You would've took her fer a burger, too."

"I ain't talkin' about food," Larsen snaps.

Shifting his weight from one large foot to the other, Porky again spits into the puddle. "Yeah. Well. Painless does have a way with the ladies."

"You sayin' I don't?"

Porky shrugs. "Naw, a'course not. That's not what I meant 'n' you know it."

Larsen sits quietly for a moment, watching the wipers swish across the windshield sporadically. "Yer right, though. About the other stuff I mean. Maybe I should settle down. That piece'a land I got? Last thing I still got that Dad left me? I should fix up the old trailer that's on it or maybe build a house. It ain't all that much, but you know, it's close to community pasture. We could run a few head a'cows..." It's not the first time he's talked about this. They both know he's more likely to lose the land in a poker game than ever build on it. Besides, for that dream to happen, he'd have to spend less time rodeoing and more time working.

But Porky just nods, and Larsen goes on.

"You come too. Partners. Maybe we should both git married, even." He shakes his head. "Lookin' back, I don't 'member it bein' so bad. Least not bad enough to split." He looks off into the dark sky for a moment before adding, "Still wonder why she did." He straightens and turns back to his friend. He reaches for the ignition, a flicker of pain crossing his face as he turns the key. Mis-matched fenders rattle as the Chevy coughs to life.

"Who in the hell would be dumb enough to marry either of us?" Porky spits. "We'd be lucky to git someone our own age, 'n' just as wore out. Yer still chasin' after young stuff. You'd never settle fer an ol' boot."

"And you would?" The truck windows are steaming up. Larsen fusses with the defrost button.

"Me, I'm more realistic. I like that Red gal; she's gittin' on but she got some good miles left in 'er yet. I think she's partial to me too 'n' she's a helluva good cook, besides. But I got nuthin' to offer her—shit. Here they come." Porky nods toward Painless and the girl, skirting puddles as they trot across the muddy exhibitor's parking lot, the rain pelting down even harder.

"Lookit that." Larsen exclaims. "We could all keep dry standin' under his beak, and he gits the girl. What really galls me, though—that fifty bucks he spotted me fer entry fees? Prob'ly comin' to collect. I was hopin' my winnings'd cover it."

"I'd've loaned it to yuh."

"Come on, Pork, you ain't got it neither."

"Well, no. But if you hadn't of turned out of them rides you would of still had a chance ..."

"I didn't turn out, I doctor-released 'n' don't go yappin' around everywhere about me turning out." Cam hisses. Then he shrugs and says, "Anyhow, the bronc I drew, even if I could hang on with my left hand, I wouldn't do much spurrin'. Goddamn bum knee actin' up, like always in this weather. Not gonna git nowhere near the kind of score I'd need. Ain't worth gittin' dumped in the mud agin just to be an also-ran. The bull's a good one, though; a spinner; might git a good score on him, but although I'm stupid as yer fond of pointin' out, I ain't stupid enough to git on him with a wrecked wrist. Pain's bad enough, I could live with that, but when it's like this I got no strength in it no matter how I tape it, like I said. Can barely pick up my rope can. And you know I ain't got a left-handed rig or glove even if I wanted to try it left-handed, which I don't. I'd be off first jump outta the gate. I'm done." He squares his shoulders and forces a neutral expression onto his face as the young couple draws up beside the truck.

"How come yer headin' out, Gobbler?" Painless asks. Pulling the brunette close, he whispers something in her ear. She giggles and looks at Larsen, then away. She has hat feathers clipped to a braid over her right ear; now rain-soaked, they leave streaks of pink and purple dye where they hang limp against her shirt. Her shirt is soaked through, clinging, and being white, almost transparent.

Larsen forces his attention from the brunette's chest to her face and nods. He removes his hat and tosses it on the dash, smiles and says, "Takin' my horse home. It's his birthday. I promised him cake 'n' ice cream." He turns his attention to his belt, works at it, and slides the buckle off. Then he turns back with a rueful smile. "Can't pay you back fer them entry fees right now, Painless, but you kin hold onto this 'til I do." He flings the buckle to the younger man. A left-handed throw, it's wide, and Painless has to let go of the girl to catch it. While he's scrambling to get it, neither of the other two cowboys takes his eyes off the brunette.

"And Painless?" Larsen continues, "be a gennelman and let Daphne wear yer coat."

"Sure thing, Gobbler." Grinning, Painless slips the buckle into the pocket of his jacket as he swings his arm back around the girl's waist. He holds up his free hand in a sort of wave, and herds the shivering girl away.

"Cam!" Porky gawps. "Ain't that yer CPRA buckle?"

"Yup. Fifteen-year-old Canadian Professional Rodeo Association All-Around Cowboy 1961 buckle just reminds everyone I'm old. Buckle ain't worth nuthin' but the silver. Kinda embarassin' really. Startin' to wear out, jus' like me. Time I quit wearin' it anyhow." He pushes at the shifter and grinds the truck into gear. "Hop in, Pork. I'll give ya a lift to yer rig."

Porky slips and slides through the mud as he makes his way around the front of the truck to the passenger side. Larsen pushes some of the clutter off the seat and onto the floor to make room for him.

"You think that young lady actually bin on a horse, Cam? I mean, ridin' with no bra-zeer and tits that size? Painful." Porky says, as he shuts the passenger door behind him.

"Didn't notice."

"Nope. Me neither." Porky agrees. "Maybe she wears a bra-zeer when she's ridin'. Still. Git 'er on a horse with a rough trot and they'd be bouncin' and a-floppin'. *That* I'd like to see."

"I didn't mind seein' 'em jus' standin' there. And I *mean* standin'. Way nicer on a cold rainy day like this than it woulda been otherwise, eh? Who knew this shittin' rain would be good fer something? But you know that smart ass cocky little shit paraded her over here just to rub my nose in it. Ain't the first time, neither."

"Ay-yuh, I know. But he ain't all that little. I wisht you wouldn't keep raggin' on him. One of these days—"

"One of these days, what? You think he'd start somethin' with *me*? Not on his own, he wouldn't. Without his big friends lookin' out fer him, he's nuthin'. He may be younger, but I could still take him, 'n' he knows it."

"I ain't gonna argue with you, buddy, but I hope we never find out." The door hadn't latched properly and slips open when Porky leans on it. He pushes it open further, spews more brown tobacco spit into the mud slime, then slams it so the latch catches. After a moment, he says, "Least she left enough buttons open a fella could git a peek at glory."

"Ay-yuh, she's a nice gal that way. Damn. Sticks in my craw, him callin' me Gobbler." Larsen fights the Armstrong steering one-handed, but the rig slews sideways in the mud before he can correct it. "Goddamn wore out tires. Why ain't they paved this lot?" He thumps the steering wheel with his good hand. "He was still in three-cornered pants when I got that nickname. Who the hell even still remembers it?"

The truck lurches through ruts and puddles, wipers slapping, small block V-8 engine grumbling about carrying a camper and pulling a loaded horse trailer through mud. Loud thumping from the horse scrambling in the trailer signals Diamond isn't happy about it either.

"Everyone calls you Gobbler, if you ain't noticed."

"Well, he ain't earned the right."

"And I expect he never will. 'Least you ain't called Porky when you ain't." Porky shakes his head slowly.

"It's just yer round face, Stu, and you *was* a li'l porker as a kid."

"Up yers." Porky growls.

"Aww, you know I don't mean nuthin'. You was just chubby. Cute chubby, like yer Ma always said. Lookin' at you now, don't think she'd even know you." Tromping the clutch, Larsen coaxes the gearshift into second, the working of his jaw proof of the pain it fires up in his wrist.

"Sure. Cute chubby. Yer an asshole, you know? I got you to thank fer makin' sure everyone calls me Porky, but you got no one but yerself to blame fer bein' called Gobbler. You always gotta have somethin' smart-ass to say."

"Yeah, well, what would you say if some shit-fer-brains sports writer asked you what you was doin' hangin' on the side of the bull?"

"Well, I wouldn't of said I was gobblin' on him."

"Naw you wouldn't, 'cause you'd-a never thought of it til the next day. Shithead shoulda knew I was havin' trouble gittin' loose bein' as he put me off away from my hand. Some sports writer. Why'd he wanna interview me anyhow? Why not interview the winner? Rodeo Today ought've canned him."

"Yeah, it ain't yer fault. Nuthin'ever is. You know they *always* interviewed you back then."

"Yeah, well, somehow they don't care so much no more. When's the last time any sports writer wanted to talk me?" Larsen scowls, then clicks his tongue. "We was the young guns then, eh, Porky? Still. Why interview a loser? Don't remember who won, maybe one of the Yanks ..."

"Dunno," Porky says. "Thought it was that kid, what's his name? From Saskatchewan. Don't think he's on the tour no more. Heard he might've got hurt. I mostly just remember how that bastard—what was that bull's name agin—Ol' Yeller?—went after you when you was on yer ass in the dirt. I thought fer sure you was gonna be killed. I'll never fergit it."

"I ain't been partial to them beige-colored spinners since then."

"Me neither, but then I ain't ridin' bulls no more. You should quit too, or at least you gotta git over that phobia you got or yer beat before you even git on one of 'em 'n' you might just as well turn out soon as you found out what you drew."

"What? And look like a pansy?"

"Not you. You'd never do nuthin' made you look like a pansy, no matter how sensible. Surprised you turned out today."

"Hsst." Cam says. "I told you—"

"I know, I know," Porky interjects. He cranks at a handle; the window squawks grudgingly and opens part way. He gets rid of his tobacco and winds the window back up. Condensation is wiped off in irregular streaks. "Anyhow, don't act like bein' called Gobbler's an insult. It ain't the worst nickname you could have. You musta heard the rumor it ain't got nuthin' to do with bull ridin' ay-tall."

"Ay-yuh," Larsen says, and chuckles. "You'd think I'd have more dates." Then the humour slides from his face. "Right after that Marie went back to her mother's."

"She never could stand to watch. That jus' done her in," Porky opines. "Plus, you *was* payin' a lot of attention to that li'l barrel racin' gal as I recall."

"That wasn't nuthin' 'n' you know it," Larsen hisses.

"Well, I got nuthin' to say about that. What matters is that Marie thought different."

Larsen glances at his friend. "You know she got hitched, eh? Marie I mean? Some big shot oil man. Big fancy house. And our kid, Lindy, all grown up, real pretty. Did I show you her pitcher?" He lifts his butt off the seat and roots in his hip pocket for his wallet. "It's last year's. Fer the school yearbook."

"Never mind haulin' it out, I seen it before once er twice er a hunnert times. Every time you git in yer cups. Yer gittin' awful goddamn maudlin, Cam."

"You and yer goddamn five-dollar words, Pork."

"Well, *some* of us finished high school. Wouldn't hurt you to expand yer vocabulary, neither." Porky shoots back. He lifts his hat and gives the top of his head a scratch before continuing: "All this reminiscin'. What's with you today? And hell yeah, she growed up pretty. Lucky fer her she took after her mother."

"She don't look nuthin' like Marie. She's got blonde hair. You even look at the pitcher?"

"You know what I mean."

"Yeah, I do." Larsen sighs. "Maybe Marie's right 'n' she don't need me. Might not even care to know me. But I'd like to see her, least once. If she don't have room fer me in her life, I'd like to hear it from her." He stomps the clutch and grimaces as he jams the gearshift into low, letting the clutch out gradually as he brakes. The engine whines. The Chevy slides to a stop near Porky's camper on the edge of the haphazard group of trucks and campers in the exhibitor's parking lot. Porky opens the door and slides out, his boots sinking in the mud.

"You stayin'?" Larsen asks.

"Dunno. Got nowhere to be before Tuesday. Think I'll stay here again tonight, hang around 'n' watch the finals, head to Jackpot tomorrow. You know the Association always puts on a nice buffet at the awards. Prob'ly roast beef 'n' so on."

"Yeah, yeah, you can't pass up all that food and a'course you wouldn't wanna miss seein' Painless scoop up the hardware, so you go right on ahead 'n' stay."

"Don't be such a mizzable bastard. Come in fer a snort before you hit the road. Maybe finish off that heel of Lemon Hart. Take the chill outta yer bones. It's early. You got plenty a time." Porky shivers. "Might be a game later."

"Not this time buddy. I got other things to do."

"Like what?"

"Just things. I gotta check in with you? I got other things goin' on in my life even if you don't. Anyhow, you know I'm skint. And yer right, I *am* a mizzable bastard. I ain't fit company. Even my horse don't like me today." Chuckling again, he shakes his head. "Really sticks in my craw, that cocky young bastard callin' me Gobbler."

"Ay-yuh, I deduced that." Knowing its reluctance to latch, Porky slams the door. The window drops three inches but the latch holds.

"See you Tuesday?" Porky shouts, raising a hand to wave.

The truck, laboring in the mire, pulls away, throaty V-8 growl irregular, windows steamy. Rain pounds down harder than before. He can't tell if his friend heard.

TWO

Calgary, Alberta

Sunday, July 18, 1976

Marie huddles in the basket chair, a forest of greenery surrounding her. This is the only place in the house where she can breathe. The only place she feels is hers. Maybe because adding this glassed-in room to Arthur's house is the only change he's allowed her to make. She even selected the furniture—nice, light rattan and wicker with colorful floral cushions—as different from the ponderous dark leather furnishings in the rest of the house as night is from day. Here her chest doesn't feel squeezed. Here she can *exist*.

There were so many things she meant to do today, things she'd put off doing yesterday, put off all week, if she's honest. Write a letter to her sister. Get groceries. Go to the liquor store. But she can't find the energy, and blames it on the rain, pattering steadily on the glass over her head, peaceful, mesmerizing. She can't force herself to get dressed and go out. *Liquor store isn't open today anyway. Definitely can't put it off another day though,* she thinks. *Tomorrow, definitely. I'll pick up the dry cleaning and Arthur's shirts, too.*

On Friday, Arthur told her he was out of shirts, all in a snit like it's up to her to keep track of how many clean ones he has left. Why did he wait until it was too late for her to do anything about it? He could've called and reminded her early in the day, or picked them up himself.

Tomorrow he'll have to wear one he's already worn once. I'll pull one out of the hamper and iron it for him. I should switch to a laundry that delivers. I'll make some phone calls tomorrow.

Today, she stayed in bed too long. She didn't want to get up at all, so being out of bed is a victory in itself. But she just pulled on stretch velour with no underwear, escaped to the atrium and then couldn't force herself to do more. All she's accomplished so far is to make coffee and sit in her big peacock chair drinking it, topping it up from time to time with Bailey's. At one point she thinks about eating something but can't decide what. So she has more coffee.

What's left of the morning evaporates as she daydreams about how things might have been, imagining herself in the arms of a man who loves her and wants her, only her in a sweet, gentle way. No matter how many other girls are around, he only has eyes for her and hugs her at every chance. Hugs, gentle hugs. There must be sex but it's not something she fantasizes about, knowing it's not his focus, but it would also be sweet and gentle with lots of love words.

At first he looks like Burt Reynolds, but with that moustache, he keeps morphing into Arthur. Arthur, with those condoms in his jacket pocket. One of his golf buddies stuck it in his pocket as a joke, and she's got some nerve snooping through his pockets, anyway. It was years ago, but she still thinks of it once in a while. She loved him then. Or did she?

She brings up a mental image of Clint Eastwood instead, but he reminds her of Lindy's father, and that's a much more painful memory than Arthur and his condoms. Cam Larsen never gave her anything but worry. Rodeo bum. Kraft dinner, bumming smokes and beer and struggling to scrape together enough money for entry fees at the next rodeo when he was between jobs or losing, or steak and lobster and drinks for everyone when he was winning or at least working, nothing in between. Long nights waiting for him when he was out somewhere playing poker. Turning a blind eye to those buckle bunnies always hanging on him. So many promises made and never kept. Not even the one about the wedding ring. The lust was searing. Undeniable. But unsustainable.

Finally, the brief, sweet hours in his arms weren't enough. He didn't try to stop her from leaving. By the time she discovered she was pregnant, he was long gone. She managed to leave a message with that friend of his—what was his name? Chubby? That's not it. Can't remember. Doesn't matter. Cam never called. How long was it before her heart quit leaping every time the phone rang?

She allows herself a couple of little cries. While she's curled up in the big chair snuffling, her cigarette somehow rolls out of the ashtray; it holds up at the edge of the glass-topped table and scorches the braided rattan trim before she notices it. *Damn it. Pull yourself together, Marie.* She sits up straighter, and pours more coffee.

The doorbell rings. She considers ignoring it but the damn thing is so loud and the ringer doesn't quit. She pulls a couple of Kleenexes from the box to wipe her eyes, then honks into them. The doorbell rings again when she's halfway there. "Patience. Patience." she mutters, but quickens her steps, crosses the foyer and pulls the door open. She draws a sharp breath when she sees it's Cam Larsen, hat in hand, under the canopy on the step.

"What are you doing here?"

"Is that any way to greet an old friend, babe?" he asks with a grin. Before she can react, he leans in and kisses her cheek, then puts his hat back on. "I just want to see my daughter."

"I told you last year, she doesn't want anything to do with you."

"I want to hear it from her. That's all. Just let her tell me."

"Sure, Cam, as soon as you pay me the child support you owe me."

"You know, I talked to a guy who knows the law. He says it don't matter I ain't paid child support. I still got rights."

"Yeah, they got a new name for guys like you. Deadbeat dads."

"Come on, babe, don't be like that."

"You had your chance years ago. You blew it."

"You know I never meant to hurt you, babe. I loved you. And you know yer way better off now than you woulda been with me. Lookit this place. And lookit you, you ain't changed at all, yer still so beautiful—"

"Don't even start that. I'm not that stupid young girl you knew, and I won't be sucked in again." She feels a rush of emotion. Her lower lip starts to quiver; she grabs it with her teeth and bites down, hoping the pain will stop her from crying again. "I gave you that picture of her last year. That's all you're going to get. Now go away and don't come back." The last comes out in a sob. She chokes it back and turns away, grabbing the edge of the door and pushing on it.

He puts up his arm to stop the door from closing, and pushes past her into the foyer. "I just want to see her. If she says she don't want me in her life, I'll go."

"She's not here. Get out. I'm going to phone the police."

"Okay," he says, and goes to the bottom of the stairs to yell up: "Lindy. Lindy." When there's no answer, he heads through the hall to the back of the house, and she hears him calling for Lindy in the kitchen and family room. He even opens the door to the stairwell and yells down into the basement before he returns to where she stands in the open doorway.

"I told you she's not here," Marie says, grateful her voice now sounds firm. "Now get out."

"I could leave a note for her but she'd never see it, would she?" He brushes past her, hops down off the step and out into the rain. "You'll be hearin' from my lawyer."

"Yeah, like you have a lawyer, big shot." she calls after him. She watches him climb into the beat-up truck parked at the curb. It emits a cloud of black smoke when the engine starts and he drives away.

She slams the door shut and leans back against it, trembling, taking gasping, heaving breaths as she tries to slow her racing heart. At last, she collects her strength and pushes away from the door; she goes to the bar in the family room, pulls a bottle of scotch out of the liquor cabinet and takes it with her into the atrium. A shot of scotch gives the Baileys coffee that little extra feel-good jolt she really needs at a time like this.

Before long she's into the second bottle of Bailey's, alarmed that somehow, more hours have slid away. No point starting anything this late, even if she had the will. As she tries to empty the second Bailey's bottle into the thermal carafe she wobbles, and the liquid runs everywhere. She gives up and pours the rest into her mug instead before settling back into her chair.

A half-empty J & B bottle and two empty Bailey's bottles seem to be staring at her, sober, unblinking judges. She can't put the empties in the garbage until the morning of garbage pick-up because Arthur might see them. She doesn't need his preaching. Especially today, what with Cam showing up like that. She should put them with the others in the trunk of her car before Arthur gets home. Damn him for finding the stash of empties in the box under the steps. What was he looking for under there, anyway? At least he'll never think of looking in her car, so really, it's a better place for them, except they rattle, so she has to make sure to get rid of them before Lindy or Jillian is with her. She doesn't need their preaching any more than Arthur's. She needs to get better at remembering to put them in the garbage after Arthur leaves on garbage day. Odd how he doesn't notice scotch bottles but a few Baileys bottles set him off. As if a little pick-me-up is a bad thing.

Is there time to take care of the bottles now? She looks at her arm and remembers her watch is still upstairs. Lindy is late, and Arthur and Jillian will be home soon, too. She'd better get a move on.

Lord knows why, but Arthur always has to pick his daughter up from her part-time job. It's raining and the streets might be slippery. Or it's too hot and her car doesn't have air conditioning. Or he wants to hit a few balls at the club so he's going that way so might as well. How he babies his grown daughter. How many cars have air conditioning, anyway? Her own doesn't, but he doesn't seem to care that she has to drive around in the heat.

Marie doesn't mind. It means he's away for hours, and it's nice having the house to herself. With no TV or stereo blaring away, she can settle in and keep the pieces of herself from floating away.

She's surprised to see a spill on her pant leg. *How did that happen without me noticing*? It was enough to have soaked through, and sticky. Her pantleg is stuck to her skin. She wipes at it with a Kleenex but gives it up as a bad job, and grips the coffee mug with both hands as though trying to prevent it from floating away, too. She thinks again, *I'll just finish this, then I'll deal with the bottles.*

She's startled by the slamming of the back door. Too late to do anything about the bottles now; the best she can do is to grab the J & B and slip it behind her chair. She hears her daughter yell out, "Mom. Mo-om."

"I'm in the atrium." she calls back. One of the Bailey's bottles has just joined the J & B when the tall, reed-thin girl bursts into the glassed enclosure. For a moment she looks at Marie, then Marie sees her scanning the mess of spilled Bailey's, the empty bottle, overflowing ashtray and the heap of used Kleenex on the table. "Mom." She draws the word out as if it has three syllables and has such a disapproving look on her face, Marie doesn't wait to hear more.

"Where have you been? You were supposed to be babysitting. Mrs. Carter called to ask if you can sit for them again on Friday night. That was hours ago. You meet up with that high school dropout again?"

"Carters came home early because of the rain, so yes, I hung out with Glen. We went to Peter's Drive-in."

"Did you park out overlooking the ravine so you could neck?"

"I've told you before, it's not like that," Lindy says, "we're just friends."

"Friends." Marie snorts, noticing a flush beginning to color Lindy's cheeks, a sure sign her daughter is lying.

"Yes, friends." Lindy drops her purse on the quarry-tiled floor with a clatter.

"You think he likes you? Maybe wants to be friends? Guys want one thing and one thing only. You think sex means something to them? It doesn't. You're no more important than a toilet."

For a heartbeat, Lindy is quiet; then she turns and goes back out to the kitchen.

"I'm talking to you." Marie calls after her. "Don't you walk away when I'm talking to you."

"I'm glad you want to talk, Mom, because I want to talk to you, too." Lindy says, returning with a mug. She fills it from the carafe. "He was here, wasn't he? Around lunch time?"

Marie nearly stops her from pouring, but it would mean a discussion about the booze and she had just barely circumvented that. But the question Lindy's asking now is something else Marie doesn't want to get into. "You should've stopped in here to let me know before you went off again. At the very least, you should've called," she says. "I was worried." She studies her daughter's face, noting high cheekbones emerging from its childish softness, realizing Lindy is on the brink of adulthood.

Lindy ignores her mother's scrutiny, sinks to the cushioned footstool, its rattan groaning as it accepts her weight, and savors the warm, creamy liquid. "Mmm. Amazing how good Bailey's tastes with a little coffee added."

At least she doesn't know about the scotch, Marie thinks.

"Have you done anything today, Mom? Besides drinking your Bailey's coffee, I mean? You haven't, have you?"

"Adults can do what they want. When you're an adult, you can, too."

"Don't worry, I won't tell Arthur," Lindy says. She clicks her tongue and heaves a sigh. "So. It *was* him, wasn't it."

"It was who?"

"The man. That cowboy. The man that was here today, in the cowboy hat. That was my dad, wasn't it. I saw him from Carter's. I saw the truck with the horse trailer in front of our house. I saw him coming away from our doorstep. I wanted to stop him from leaving, but by the time I was out the door, he was driving away and I couldn't catch up." She deposits her mug on the table and folds her long legs under her. Then her shoulders droop and her voice softens. "I guess he didn't see me."

"I don't know why you'd call the man who fathered you your *dad*." Marie snaps.

"So," Lindy says, picking up her mug again. "So, I guess since he was here, he actually does want to see me after all."

"Did I say it was him? Why would he show up here after all these years? Plus, he doesn't know where we live."

"He does know. Grammy said she told him."

"Did she? Well, I wouldn't believe everything *she* says. And anyway, *if* he got in touch with her, the only reason would be to ask for money."

"No, he didn't ask for money, he asked about you, and she told him about me."

"Well, if that's true, he was just faking it, you know, idle conversation working up to asking for money. Wouldn't be the first time he conned your grandmother into giving him money. And he's *never* contacted me. That man you saw today, he was just a grubby old creep wanting to sharpen knives."

"But he had a horse trailer."

"Well..." Marie raises her mug and drinks deeply, mind racing, searching for an answer to that. "Horse trailer? I thought it was a tool trailer."

"So. He wanted to sharpen knives, but only stopped at our house."

"How do you know he didn't go to our neighbours?" Marie pretends interest in something out the window over Lindy's head.

Lindy's eyes narrow. "Well, he didn't come to Carter's."

Marie very nearly relents. Should she tell her? Damn her mother for telling him about Lindy. And did she have to give him her address and phone number? She never had a good word to say about him. *"You see him through rose-colored glasses. Movie star good looks doesn't make him good husband material, and he has no prospects. He's nothing but a good time Charlie. He'll leave you crying."* Why would she help him find her? How would Lindy benefit from knowing her father, a rodeo rider who never did an honest day's work in his life? She harps on about how Lindy has a right to know her father, but it's not up to her to make that decision.

He showed up last year during Stampede week, too. Both times by sheer coincidence no one else was home. Last year she gave him Lindy's school picture, told him Lindy wanted nothing to do with him and that he should respect Lindy's decision and stay away. Yet this year he landed on the doorstep again.

He's right, though; she's done okay all these years without him, better than if they were still together. She won't let him barge into her life—into their lives—now.

Her moment of indecision past, she draws herself up and gets to her feet. "Come on, honey. Unless you're coming with us, I'll make you something for dinner. Hamburger Helper, maybe?"

Lindy stands, makes a face, and shakes her head. "It's okay, Mom. I'll do it. Are you going out?"

"Stampede party. I told you about it, didn't I?" Marie forces a smile onto her face and cheerfulness into her voice. "It's at DeWitt's. You girls are welcome to come along. You remember, we can see the fireworks from their deck. You know what a big display they have on closing night. Everyone will be in jeans but mine are all so uncomfortable. I have to shop for new ones I guess, but for tonight, I'll wear the white square dance dress and my cowboy boots. That and my white cowboy hat should do it."

"Oh god. DeWitt's?"

"Of course, DeWitt's. I told you about it weeks ago."

"I didn't think we'd be going, though."

"We're lucky to be invited. Why wouldn't we go? She drops her voice conspiratorially. "Arthur's in line for a promotion. He thinks Hal might make the announce tonight. Er, announcement. Announce it tonight. Besides. You always enjoy their barbeques."

"What makes you think that? I tolerated them, but I haven't *enjoyed* being anywhere near him since he grabbed my ass."

"Lindy. Don't you *dare* make up stories. Saying things like that can ruin lives."

"I'm not making it up. I told you about it. I've steered clear of him ever since. He thinks he's sexy but he's so creepy—always standing too close. That sweaty, oily forehead pressing against yours when he hugs you. Accidentally sliding his hand over your ass. Ugg."

"He's just friendly. Don't you know when someone's just being friendly? Sometimes I wish you were more like Jillian. She likes him."

"Come on, Mom. Why don't you believe me? He's not *just friendly*, he's creepy. He gets away with it because he's the boss. You know I'm telling the truth. He does the same thing to everyone, to Jillian, too. And you can't have missed how he drools over your boobs." She straightens, then cocks her head and studies her mother through narrowed eyes. "My God. You *like* it."

Marie's hand strikes with resounding suddenness. Red streaks blossom on Lindy's cheek. For a long moment neither speaks or moves.

Then Lindy bolts, racing across the foyer to the stairway. Taking two steps at a time, she disappears into the upper hall and in a heartbeat, Marie hears her bedroom door slam.

Another fight with my daughter. Somehow lately our conversations always become shouting matches. Still, I shouldn't have done that, Marie thinks. *I don't know why I did.*

She starts after her, but just then, Arthur and Jillian bustle in from the garage, filling the entryway. Arthur shrugs his jacket onto the newel post at the bottom of the stairs.

"Traffic was unreal. Just unreal. Every year I swear we should leave town for Stampede Week." He gives Marie a perfunctory peck. "Thank god it's over for another year."

Jillian slams the garage door behind her and snorts as she dumps her shopping bags on the hall stand. "I see you didn't bother to get dressed again today, Marie."

"Jillian." Arthur warns. He loops an arm around Marie and propels her down the hall toward the family room.

"I thought I'd make Hamburger Helper for the girls, if they don't want to go with us. Lindy says she doesn't. What about you, Jillian?"

"Maybe," Jillian says.

Marie starts to turn toward the kitchen, but Arthur tows her down the three steps into the family room.

"You like Hal, don't you, Jillian?" Arthur says.

"He's nice. He's going to get me a job as soon as one comes available. Maybe in the steno pool. Don't worry, it won't be on the same floor you work on, Dad." Jillian replies. "But my friends might want to go do something down at the Stampede, so I might not go with you. Is there anything to eat here?"

"Hamburger Helper," Marie says. "At least I think there's a package of hamburger in the freezer."

"Agggh. Not again." Jillian groans.

"I'll leave you some money so you can order a pizza," Arthur offers; then he turns to Marie and says, "in the meantime, we'll just enjoy a little peace and quiet. A nice scotch. Then we'll go up and get in a nap before we have to get ready for dinner." He leans in and winks. "Okay?"

Marie hopes her grimace looks like a smile and wishes she'd made up the bed before he got home. Not that a tidy bed would be a deterrent. She remembers the joke she and her college friends thought was so funny: you know why the bride in wedding photos is always smiling? Because she'll never have to give another blow job. Back then, she thought nobody would ever do such a thing anyway, so it was funny on two levels. Now she knows it really is a joke. Just not a funny one.

Following them into the family room, Jillian loosens her hair from its clips and shakes it. Falling around her shoulders in a dark cloud, it frames her fine features. Dark brows. Porcelain white skin in the winter, beautifully tanned in summer thanks to the hours she spends laying in the sun. Elizabeth Taylor to Lindy's Grace Kelly. She's looking at Marie with a sweet smile that reminds Marie of the little girl. She smiles back. Then, in a sugary tone, Jillian says, "Gain any more weight, Marie, and you'll need a whole new collection of velour lounging suits."

Arthur turns toward his daughter as if to say something but she gives him a hard glare; he shrugs and turns away, saying nothing. Then with a smug expression and a flounce, Jillian leaves the family room.

Arthur sighs and draws Marie into his arms. "She had a tough day, Marie, thanks to that bitchy supervisor," he says. "She doesn't mean anything." Holding her at arm's length, he chucks her under the chin and runs a manicured forefinger along her nose. "Okay?"

Tough day at McDonald's? Really? It obviously didn't stop her from shopping.

If only they had sold this monstrous house and bought their own years ago. Something smaller, with no basement suite, so his daughter would move out. Maybe then the marriage wouldn't have deteriorated to what it is now. When she first suggested it, Arthur wouldn't discuss it. The last time she tried to talk to him, insisting, he exploded. That dining chair couldn't be repaired, and it was four hundred dollars to fix the drywall.

Marie has no more fight in her. She thinks about leaving but hasn't figured out how to do it. Maybe she'll do it when Lindy's away at school. She will. She'll leave him when Lindy's away. *If* he sets up that annuity to cover her tuition as he promised. She'll plan for it. Start her own bank account; tell him she needs more money for the household budget, and make sure some of it goes into her own account every week so she has enough to live on for a few months in case he's nasty about alimony. Until then, she has to accept the reality the first wife will never be truly buried, endure Jillian, and go along with whatever Arthur wants. *Sure, Jillian, go ahead and insult me. Sure, Arthur, go ahead and defend your daughter when she insults me, you can still have your weekly blow job.* She bobs her head.

"Good." He presses his lips to the bridge of her nose, his moustache prickly. "As long as we're talking about it, though, Jillian does have a point about your weight, Marie. You need exercise. Why did you quit going to squash? Why don't you sign up again?"

Because I hate it? Marie thinks. But she clenches her jaw and shrugs.

"I'll sign you up next time I go to the club. Now you sit, and let's have that scotch. I can use it. Damned MacLeod Trail was a nightmare." Rolling up his sleeves, he turns away and busies himself at the liquor cabinet, whistling tunelessly. He's never more cheerful than when there's a blow job on the horizon.

Scotch on the rocks, Marie thinks. *Not rum and coke, or rye and ginger, or god forbid, a White Russian. No chance it could be something that tastes good.* She first drank it when she started dating Arthur, taking her cue from what the other bigwigs' wives ordered. He never mentioned it, but she could tell by his slight nod that he approved. By the time she no longer cared whether he approved or not, she had learned to appreciate it. It's a nice boost for the Bailey's and on its own, the buzz is more immediate and intense. It makes up for the taste. She'll take the scotch with her when they go upstairs.

She sinks into an armchair and closes her eyes, listening to the sounds of Arthur getting the drinks. Then, she doesn't think about how to leave, how to get out of playing squash, or the looming blow job. Instead, she re-lives the hot rush that swept over her when she saw Cam on the doorstep, hat in hand. It was as if twenty years evaporated and she was once again the girl he picked out of so many. Does he have to look the way he does? Still tough and lean. Cocky. But for the crow's feet and frown lines between his brows, he might have been the twenty-something she fell so hard for. Narrow hips in tight jeans. Belly washboard flat. Hair receding slightly and darkening, but still thick, if too short to be in style. Still clean shaven despite moustaches being so popular even Arthur had grown one.

She hadn't been able to say any of the things she'd fantasized. He'd been aggressive, sure, but that kiss. Calling her Babe, as he had in the old days. Saying he loved her back then with that huskiness in his voice was almost enough to make her think he might still have feelings for her. That something might still be possible between them. How easily he made her heart race. She would never want anything permanent with him, but maybe a few stolen moments?

When she has to go upstairs with Arthur, she'll take fantasies of Cam Larsen along with the scotch.

With a sharp intake of breath, she gives herself a mental shake. She pushes thoughts of Cam, Jillian, Lindy, and the nap out of her mind. She makes a mental promise that if Lindy doesn't come down before they leave, she will apologize first thing in the morning.

Then she feels another little piece of herself float away as she focuses on that mellow liquid, the golden elixir that's all Arthur can offer to warm her. In the glass he's holding out to her.

THREE

Calgary, Alberta

Sunday, July 18, 1976

When she hears her mother and Arthur leave, Lindy goes through their room and into the closet, where she rummages through the pockets of all of Arthur's suits. Then she checks his jackets in the entry closet and his home office. He usually has at least one or two ten dollar bills (he hates twenties) and lots of change in his pants pockets. She isn't disappointed. She doesn't take all the change, just the quarters and fifty cent pieces, and she even leaves a five dollar bill so he won't think he's been cleaned out. It's likely an unnecessary precaution as he probably never knows for sure how much money he has in his pockets; after all, he brags that it takes him three weeks to cycle through his suits. Maybe he won't even miss it. Or if he does, he'll think her mother took it. Wouldn't be the first time he's accused her of going through his pockets. She experiences a twinge of guilt about that.

Her mother took her purse with her of course, but there's often cash left in the others; she roots through them and comes up with a couple of two-dollar bills and a fiver, and more small change.

Jillian's car is still in its spot next to the garage, but that doesn't mean she's home, because she could have been picked up by friends and Lindy wouldn't have heard her leave when she was upstairs. Lindy goes down to Jillian's suite to check. The door is locked as always, but Lindy learned long ago that it's simple to pick with a bobby pin. She listens and hears Jillian's voice. She's still home, talking on her private line. "Rats." she mutters under her breath. Besides the loose change in her purses, Miss Perfect Jillian Jones usually has a few bucks tucked away with her condoms in a makeup bag in the back of the under-sink cabinet of her ensuite.

The first time Lindy found that stash, she wasn't looking for money. She was just snooping as she's done for years whenever Jillian could be counted on to be away for a few hours. Her quest: Jillian's birth control pills. Not that she'd tell anyone, but to prove to herself Jillian's perfect virtuous daughter image was a pretense. She was surprised on two counts: one, that she would rely on condoms; and two, earlier, Jillian claimed she was broke. She begged Arthur for money so she could go out with her friends and he gave her two ten dollar bills. Twenty dollars. Two full days of babysitting pay, just for the asking.

Every time Jillian whines about not having money, Arthur can be counted on to go into his "you girls have to learn to budget" lecture, always including Lindy even though it's Jillian who always claims she's broke. In the end, he gives Jillian what she wants. Lindy tried Jillian's tactics, but after getting the lecture and only a couple of dollars for the third time, she didn't ask again. She can get two bucks out of his pockets any time and doesn't have to endure his lecture. It's stealing, but justifiable. Sort of an equalization payment.

Lindy has never said anything about the condoms, because if she did, she'd have to admit she was snooping. Better that Jillian doesn't know she knows about them. She harbors the idea that if Jillian ever really pisses her off, she'll take a fine needle to every condom in the pack, see how long it takes her to get pregnant. Will she still be Miss Perfect Jillian Jones then?

She's never taken any of the money, either, but likes knowing about it. Unlike the niggling guilt she feels when she steals from her parents, she'd have no qualms about stealing Jillian's stash should the need arise.

Who would Jillian tell? Unfortunately, tonight's the first time the need has arisen, Jillian is still home, and she doesn't have time to wait for her to go.

She trots back upstairs and as she's going through the kitchen, spots the pizza money Arthur left on the counter. It is just good fortune she came into the kitchen before Jillian had a chance to scoop it up, because Jillian would go for pizza, all right, but with her friends, not with Lindy. She has a mental movie of Jillian totally flipping out when she emerges from her lair and can't find the pizza money. Maybe she'll think Arthur forgot to leave it and she'll be furious with him. If only she could be there to witness it! But by the time she screams at him about it and they realize Lindy took it, she'll be long gone.

Even without an involuntary contribution from Jillian, between the remains of her allowance, money from babysitting earlier, the pizza money and the pilfering, she has plenty of cash. She suffers another pang of guilt. This is beyond equalizing, it's stealing on a larger scale. But for years, curiosity about her birth father has been niggling at her. When asked, her mother gets mad, something she's been doing more often lately, and goes off on a tirade about how the only person he ever cared about is himself. *He never wanted a kid. What makes you think he wants you? He doesn't. Don't waste your time even thinking about him.*

She can't quit thinking about him, though. Grammy will at least talk about him. Tell her about things he did. What he was like. She even has newspaper clippings from way back and says instead of being ashamed of him, he's someone to brag about. Besides being a champion, he's also charming and good-looking. She says lots of marriages don't work out and that Lindy must have friends whose parents are divorced. Sure, her mother was never married to her father, but people no longer care about that so much, and if it bothers her, she doesn't need to tell anyone. The important thing is that Lindy was born and she is loved.

That's nice. But it doesn't answer Lindy's questions about her paternal relatives. What are her other biological grandparents like? And she might have another whole set of cousins. Grammy agrees Lindy should know about them; they're her family after all. And what if they'd like to know Lindy? Don't they have the right?

Grammy said that when her father phoned, despite knowing Marie would object, she told him about Lindy. He asked for their address and phone number. Does that sound like someone who doesn't want anything to do with her?

Her last name is Jones because Arthur adopted her when she was too young to object, maybe because her mother didn't want to keep explaining why Lindy had a different last name. She likely wouldn't have objected anyway, at least not until she started imagining her birth father so much and thinking she'd rather have her birth father's name. Lindy Larsen has a nice ring to it. Larsen sounds like it could be Swedish or maybe Norwegian, and Lindy thinks she looks Scandinavian. She definitely doesn't take after her mother's side of the family; they're originally from Italy, dark-haired and olive-skinned. She's much taller than her mother and grandmother, taller than her grandfather, even, and she's the only one of her cousins with blonde hair. Her mother thinks she should be happy knowing she's fifty percent Italian and one hundred percent third-generation Canadian, but more and more over the last few years, she's yearned to know about the other half. The only way for her to find out is from her father. And now for the first time, she knows where he is. She has a chance to find him but has to do it now because, in a few weeks, she's leaving. When she's home again next summer, he might not be here. So stealing money and running away is justified. Necessary.

Because she doesn't want her mother to report her missing, she writes a note:

Mom:

I'm going to find my dad. Don't worry, I'll be fine. See you in a week or so.

Lindy.

She dons her most western, Stampede-week-looking shirt and packs panties, toothbrush, a pack of Tampax and a deodorant stick in her biggest purse. She takes nylon Baby Dolls instead of pyjamas because they scrunch down to almost nothing and her purse is already nearly bursting. On impulse, she picks up the half-read paperback copy of *Carrie* off her night table, thinking it will be nice to have something to read if she has to wait while her father does rodeo stuff, but then she can't close the purse. She goes to the closet where a calendar marking her periods hangs, and decides to turf out the pack of Tampax, keeping just a couple. If she gets a nasty surprise, she can always buy another pack. Now she can close the purse, just barely. She zips it, slides the strap onto her shoulder and trots downstairs.

In the atrium, she surveys the mess. Her mother must have had quite a day. From the looks of it she smoked a full pack. Besides the empty Bailey's bottle on the table, there are bottles half-hidden behind her mother's favourite chair. She shakes her head. *If you drank all that, no wonder you were so cranky,* she thinks. *Oh, Mom. Too bad your backbone disappears when Arthur's around.*

She props the note up against the empty Bailey's bottle on the table. No one will be going into the atrium until morning at the earliest, so the note won't be found too soon. Then, she slips out the front door, a bounce in her step as she trots to the bus stop a block away. Like a sign her quest is meant to be, the bus comes trundling up the hill mere moments after she gets there. She climbs aboard, filled with euphoria in the knowledge she's on her way to Stampede Park to meet her father for the first time.

The new city bylaw allows stores to be open Sundays and stay open late during Stampede, so Western Outfitters across the street from Stampede Park is still bustling with tourists. Full of optimism and with a load of unexpected cash thanks to the pizza money, she goes in, tries on boots and settles on a brown suede pair. The sales girl assures her suede is the latest craze and everyone wants suede boots now. She likes them for the colorful flower inlays on the tops. Of course, she also needs a Calgary Stampede white cowboy hat. Thus outfitted and feeling very rodeo cowgirl-ish, she tosses her running shoes in the first garbage can she comes to.

It costs more to get into the fairgrounds than she expected. Everything costs more than expected. A lousy burger and fries is four dollars and doesn't even come with a drink. Still, since they never did get that pizza, she had no dinner. It was worth it, though, imagining how pissed off Jillian would be when she emerged from her lair in the basement to discover there was no pizza money. She may have to make a sandwich, or dip into that stash of hers. But it means Lindy also hasn't eaten, not since being at Peter's with Glen, and then she only had a milkshake. If she'd been smart, she would've made herself a sandwich before leaving the house, but she was mission-focused and couldn't tolerate the delay. Now she is ravenous. She gets the burger even though it depletes her funds. She isn't concerned, certain she'll connect with her father before long.

She makes her way through the midway to the rodeo grounds, but after wandering around long enough to get a look at all the cowboy-types, realizes there's no one that looks like the faded black-and-white photo hidden in her mother's underwear drawer. Approaching strangers is daunting, especially since it's getting dark and the corrals aren't well lit, but she gathers her courage and after the first couple of times, it becomes easier. But not productive. The men all know Cam Larsen, but to a man, they don't know where he is. They suggest other places for her to look, and she exhausts them all with no luck.

At last one of the younger cowboys she approaches tells asks if she's checked the Cantina.

"Cantina? You mean, like a restaurant? Like in the Agriplex?"

"No, it's off by itself."

"I didn't see anything like that."

"You wouldn't, I suppose. It's off by itself, like I said. It's mostly just jockeys and rodeo people go there. You could try looking there."

"This late?"

"This ain't too late. Maybe too early, even. Guys go there for a midnight snack before turning in. And fer breakfast. They got this awesome breakfast sandwich, sausage and bacon and an egg in there, some cheese too, and sauce, special sauce. Mmmm-mmm-mmm. I'd come here just fer that if I..."

Lindy must be giving him a who-gives-a-fart look as he stops mid-sentence, tips his hat, and says "Well, good luck" before striding off. He's merged into the midway crowd before she realizes he didn't tell her where "off by itself" the cantina is.

She passes a building housing public washrooms, and ducks in to relieve her bladder. When she comes out of the stall, there are three girls in fancy Stampede wear at the sinks, touching up their makeup. Their lacey, ruffle-trimmed western shirts and yoke-backed bell bottoms; wide, tooled belts with beautiful silver buckles; and hats adorned with brightly-colored feathers put her outfit to shame. Even with the embroidery on the yoke, her shirt is plain compared to their pretty, feminine ones. She doesn't even have a belt. Most Calgarians have a hat and a shirt and maybe boots, but these girls look like they might be more than just Stampede Week cowgirls.

She waits for her turn at the sink. When they turn to leave, the dark-haired girl makes eye contact with Lindy and nods.

"Hi," Lindy replies. Then she realizes there's no reason to ask only cowboys about her father. "Say, I'm looking for someone. He's a rodeo rider. I wonder if you might know where he'd be."

"Well," the cowgirl responds, "we know pretty well all the rodeo people. What's his name?"

"Cam Larsen."

"Of course we know him," one of the other girls pipes up. "Everyone knows him."

"Oh great." Lindy says. "Do you know where he is?"

"Dunno where he is, for sure, but if we were looking for him, we'd check the stock corrals, maybe around the back of the chutes. Over where the exhibitor viewing area is. You know, on the opposite side of the infield from the grandstand, where the little bleachers are?"

"I've been over behind the chutes, but didn't pay much attention, I guess. I didn't see bleachers."

They give her directions, and wishing her luck, leave. She follows them out of the washrooms. It's full dark now and the thought of wandering around out there by herself where anything could be concealed in the shadows gives her the heebie-jeebies. *Don't be such a baby,* she tells herself, and turns in the direction the girls indicated.

When it's nearly midnight and she's slogged through mud and manure and got a sliver from grabbing a corral fence and still hasn't found him, disappointment washes over her. She pushes it away, telling herself to stay positive. There is still one more possibility: the cantina that young cowboy told her about. If she can find it before the whole place closes up.

She presses through the dwindling crowd around the Crown and Anchor game. The mouse game, Pineapple Freeze stand, corn dog truck and the cotton candy stands have already closed. The smell of dog shit seems to be following her; she goes closer to a street light so she can see and confirms there's something dark squished onto the bottom of her left boot. It's not mud.

"Shit." Literally. She tries scraping it off on the edge of the asphalt walkway and gets most of it, but there's still some she'd need a stick to deal with. She finds a discarded popsicle stick and uses that, careful not to get anything on her hands, but the cleanup will take more. Hopefully she'll find some grass to scuff it off on. Right now, no suitable grass patches present themselves.

Feet on fire, cursing her new cowboy boots and the dog shit, she leans against the wall of a concrete block building. Her purse seems to be getting heavier by the minute and the strap feels like it's wearing a groove in her shoulder. She sets it down on the asphalt beside her feet. How many miles has she walked, combing the venues where her father might be? Should have been? All the people she asked, and still nothing. She hadn't expected it would take this long to find him. But maybe it's not surprising she can't find the man since she can't even find the cantina.

She's about to admit defeat and turn back when the girls she met in the washroom a few hours earlier come along the path toward her. They recognize her and stop.

"Oh, hi. Did you find Cam?"

Lindy shakes her head. "I was told he might go to the cantina, but I haven't even been able to find it."

"Well, he might go there, all right. And you almost found it. It's just around the corner. We're heading there now. Why don't you come with us?"

"Thanks," Lindy says.

"I'm Carla. This is Judy, and Renee."

"Lindy."

"It's not much further, Lindy," Carla says.

Lindy walks with them; when they pass the end of the concrete block building and turn right, she sees "CANTINA" in big red letters on a white awning a few hundred yards farther on. Inside the tent is a huddle of folding tables and chairs with what must be the food prep area hidden behind a small counter.

There are few customers, and only four that look like cowboys. Carla says to Lindy, "I don't see him here. Come on, we'll ask those guys if they know where he is."

Once greetings are over, Carla asks the men, "You guys know where Larsen is?".

"Why d'you care, honey? He ain't got nuthin' I ain't got, as you well know." The nearest man says. Everyone chuckles. He loops an arm around her and pulls her down into his lap.

"Not for me, silly," Carla says with a giggle as she points at Lindy. "*She's* looking' for him."

All eyes turn toward Lindy.

"I seen him buzzin' around Daphne at breakfast," one of the other cowboys says. "Don't know that any of you gals'll rope him tonight. Might as well stick with us."

The cowboys all agree; everyone but Lindy chuckles, Judy and Renee slide into laps, leaving one cowboy sitting alone. He eyes Lindy, gets to his feet and smiles as he takes her hand, saying, "How do, little lady. My name's Alf."

"Lindy," she says, giving his hand a shake.

He doesn't release her hand after the shake. Instead, he says, "Why don't you and me get to know each other better, Lindy?"

Lindy draws a quick breath and pulls her hand away; she shakes her head and says, "Ummm, no thanks. I have to... I'm just..." She backs a couple of steps away.

Carla says, "She's not lookin' to party tonight, Alf, not with you, anyway. She's looking for Larsen, like I told you." The other girls giggle; Alf shrugs. Then as if they all heard some secret command, Carla's group gets up and heads away. Carla, tucked under the cowboy's arm, looks at Lindy and says, "Bye. Good luck." Lindy catches a glimpse of a wedding band as the man's hand cups her breast.

Odd Carla didn't introduce him as her husband, Lindy thinks. Still, it's nice how friendly the girls are, even bringing her along to the Cantina and introducing her to their boyfriends, or in Carla's case, husband. She was even welcome to join them, and she might have. That Alf guy was older, but kind of cute. But he thought she'd sit on his lap like the other girls were doing even though she'd just met him? Cute, but too forward. Besides, the table was already crowded and she needs space, an extra chair, for when her father comes.

She chooses a table with the least dried-on condiments; it's also furthest away from the only other customers, half a dozen rough-looking men. Crappy as the place is and despite the questionable character of the only other customers, it's a relief to be off her feet.

Loud laughter erupts from the men. *They're probably the guys who work the rides,* she thinks. They have noticed her. Something about the way they look at her makes her stomach shrivel. She's relieved when they get up and leave.

As they're leaving, a different group of cowboys straggles in. She recognizes one from when she approached him earlier. He nods to her and tips his hat. *Must be a cowboy thing,* she thinks. An old-fashioned gesture, but nice.

Now that she's seen the place, Lindy concludes cowboys care more about the price of the food than the cleanliness of the kitchen it's made in. She can't imagine eating anything made here, but what matters is that cowboys are still coming in. Maybe Cam Larsen will show up too. If she doesn't find him tonight, she won't be here for that fabulous breakfast sandwich, special sauce notwithstanding.

"You gotta order somethin' or let someone else have the table."
A big-bellied man with tattooed arms and soiled bib apron finally
acknowledges her, calling out across empty tables as he wipes at the
counter.

As if tables are in big demand. Lindy considers going to wait
outside, but with her feet as burning and sore as they are, decides
against it. "Uhh...Pepsi, please." She removes her hat and careful to
select a clean spot, sets it and her purse on the table.

"Coke okay?"

"That's fine."

"Small? Mejum? Large?"

"Umm," she's able to read the menu from where she sits, and studies
it while the waiter taps his fingers on the counter. The price of a large
soft drink is seventy cents, pretty steep, but she's really thirsty and it's
still within her budget. She says, "Umm, large please, and lots of ice."

"Uh-huh." He grunts and turns away.

Lindy struggles to remove her boots, cursing them again. The
flimsy folding chair squawks and jiggles so dramatically she's afraid
it might collapse. But since she's seen chairs just like these hold a
full-grown man with a girl in his lap, they must be okay. It holds, and
she succeeds in getting her boots off.

Buying those was just one of the stupid things I did today, she thinks.
Five hours ago, she thought they were so pretty. Now? She curses her
stupidity in buying the eight-and-a-halfs instead of the size nines she
usually wears, thinking it would make her feet look small. She pulls off
her socks and stuffs them into the boots, savoring the cool night air
washing over her feet.

The waiter calls out, "Yer drink, miss." He's standing behind the
counter, making no move to bring it to her.

*Have to order something or leave the table, but no table service? What
a crappy place.* Lindy sighs and gets to her feet. She looks around and
seeing no one close, puts her hat on the seat of the chair and pushes

it in, hiding both the boots and the hat. Swinging her purse onto her shoulder, she picks her way across the asphalt. "*Gahh*," she mutters as she steps in something sticky. At the counter, she digs her last two dollar bill out of her purse and hands it to the waiter. He takes it with a grunt and turns away, disappearing into the back.

"Hey. My change." Lindy calls after him.

He comes partway back and jabs his pudgy forefinger up at a faded sign half hidden by a bare yellow bulb. Squinting, Lindy makes out the words: "Table minimum $2 per person".

"Son of a bitch," she mutters. *There goes my bus fare home,* she thinks, panic rising. *I better find him tonight.* She picks up the drink and retraces her steps to her table, avoiding the sticky puddle.

Another handful of cowboys saunters in and clusters around the order window. She recognizes one she talked to earlier. He's standing next to the tallest one, who has his back to her. From the back, they all look kind of the same, but this one is wearing a cowboy hat like the one her father wore when she saw him at her house. It could be him.

The one she spoke to earlier looks her way, then says something to the tall man. He turns. He has high cheekbones and a prominent nose, reminding her of a predatory bird. The photo in her mother's underwear drawer is slightly out of focus and part of his face is in the shadow of his hat, but it's still obvious he's better looking than this guy, besides being older.

Lindy sighs and studies her drink. She sips the Coke. It's watery. If that's any indication, this place can't possibly have the best food at the fair. She presses her burning soles onto the cool pavement, ignoring the stickiness, and thinks about putting some of the ice from her drink on her feet. How much longer should she wait? When does this place close up for the night? Where will she go if they kick her out and she hasn't found her father yet?

The scraping of a chair being pulled away from the table startles her, and she looks up to find the tall cowboy with the prominent nose standing beside her. A bulging denim crotch and a huge, ornate silver buckle are at eye level.

"Evenin', miss," he says, his voice soft and oddly musical. "Mind if I set?"

Before she can answer, he slides onto the chair at her elbow; Lindy finds herself looking into striking green-yellow eyes and is at a loss for words. "There's a two dollar minimum," is all she can think of, and points at the sign.

He barks a laugh, waves at the man with the tattooed arms and holds up two fingers. The waiter nods, turns to the order window, and calls out "Two specials."

Once she's gathered her wits, she says, "You can't sit here. I'm waiting for someone."

"So I hear." His even white teeth gleam and his odd, multi-color eyes seem to change and become more hazel. She realizes with a start that he'd be attractive if it wasn't for that nose, and forces herself to look away.

"Yer gonna have a long wait."

"What do you mean?"

"You bin askin' about a buddy of mine."

"Cam Larsen is your buddy?"

"Yup. My name's Nick," he says, and sticks out his hand.

"Lindy," she replies, taking his hand for a quick shake. Craning her neck, she surveys the tables again. "Is he with you? Where is he?"

"Why're you lookin' fer him?"

Sighing, Lindy rests her head on the tent pole behind her. "Like I told your friend earlier, it's personal."

"Hmm." His eyes, now more olive green than yellow or hazel, flash at her. "Well, Linda, I might know where he is—"

"It's Lindy, not Linda. And you might know where he is? Do you or don't you?" Then she sits back again with another sigh. "I'm sorry. That was uncalled for. It's been a long, crappy day."

"Apology accepted," Nick says, still grinning. "I said I might know where he is," he continues, "but I definitely know where he ain't, and that's here. He pulled out this mornin'. So he's on the road somewhere. Or camped somewhere. Or maybe at his place by now."

"Oh, his place? Where he lives? Where's that?"

"Dunno exactly, somewhere's around Maple Creek. Course, he could also pick up a few days' work somewhere too. He could do that and still get to the next rodeo."

"Oh, of course. Of course, he'd be going to the next rodeo. Where is it?"

"Now that I don't know. There's not just one *next one*, eh? There's a few to choose from 'pendin' on where he figgers he'll do the best. Maybe the one with the most prize money." He raises his voice to get the attention of the other men he'd come in with, now seated at the next table. "Hey, any you guys seen Porky?"

They all shake their heads and mutter.

"Porky?" Lindy queries.

"Yeah, Porky and Gob...er, Larsen, are like this," he crosses his middle finger over his index. "Close. He'll know where Larsen was headin' if anyone does. But I ain't seen Porky since the awards neither. He likely headed out, too."

The waiter who wouldn't bring her drink to the table now arrives with the two cheeseburger specials. Nick passes him a ten dollar bill and tells him to keep the change. Then he pushes one of the paper-lined baskets at Lindy, takes the lid off one of the drinks and turns to his friends at the next table and asks, "Who's got my rye?" The nearest cowboy hands him the bottle. He twists the lid off and pours a shot into his drink. "You want yours fixed up?" he asks.

"Umm, no thanks," Lindy says, "I gotta go."

He shrugs, screws the lid on the bottle and passes it back to his friend. Then he rips ketchup pouches open and slathers his fries. He eats a few, then picks up his burger and digs in.

"About the next rodeo?"

"I'd be guessin'," he drawls, between bites.

"Well, how many rodeos can there be?"

"More than you might think. Hunnerds, if you count the U.S. But he's likely headin' to the same one we're goin' to. Not that big, but it's on the tour."

"Which is...?"

"High Prairie."

"High Prairie? Where's that?"

"North west of Edmonton. Up Grande Prairie way."

"Okay, thanks." Lindy pulls her socks out of her boots and sticks her feet in them, then tries to pull the first boot on. Her foot only goes as far as the shaft and seems stuck there, as if it's now a full size too small.

"You hitchhikin'?"

She wouldn't hitchhike. But what business is it of his? Lindy focuses her attention on her boots, ignoring the question while she thinks about her options. She's never tried hitchhiking, not even with a friend, but she doesn't have a car and neither Jillian nor her mother would lend theirs. Not that she'd ask. Maybe one of her friends would be up for a road trip.

But she has tonight to worry about before figuring out how to get to High Prairie next weekend. She still has a dime for the payphone, but to call someone, even Karen? At this hour? If anyone answered, it would be Karen's mother; she'd be annoyed and would hang up. Dime gone.

Glen won't come tonight, wouldn't even hear the phone from his basement bedroom. And he has to work so he won't be able to take her to High Prairie next week.

She has to go home tonight, and try for High Prairie next weekend, maybe with Karen, maybe by Greyhound, or maybe she'll even try hitchhiking. But what if she can't sneak out again? What if her mother has already found the note? She'll flip out. Plus, after emptying all of Arthur's pockets today, there will be slim pickings next week. If Jillian has to work on Friday, she can steal her secret stash; otherwise, she'll have to take money out of her savings account. She's been saving to buy a car for a couple of years now; normally she wouldn't touch that, but this is an emergency.

Hovering over his cheeseburger special, Nick scarcely looks up as he says, "Might as well ride with me. I got room." He points at her cheeseburger. "You gonna eat that?"

She pushes it over to him. Ride with him? Really? Could she do that? Take a ride, spend a week maybe, with an older guy, someone she doesn't even know? But if she doesn't, will she get to High Prairie at all? Or find Cam Larsen on her own? What if he isn't at the High Prairie rodeo? Where would she go from there? And how would she get there anyway?

Unless she goes with this guy, she likely won't be able to find him, at least not this summer. She only has these few weeks. A renewed sense of urgency washes over her. She'll walk home now. Should be able to make it by three. If her mother hears her come in, she'll weather the tongue lashing, pretend to be contrite, apologize up and down, maybe cry a little. If she plays her cards right, she can probably even make her mother feel guilty— blame her—thanks to that slap. If her mother sucks up enough, she'll forgive her, tell her she's sorry and that it was partly her fault too; that she changed her mind and came home because leaving like that, making her mother worry, was wrong.

And for money, her mother always leaves her purse on the hall table. She must have cash. As soon as her mother goes back to bed, she'll sneak out before anyone else is up and come back here as soon as the buses are running. Because it's obvious her best option is to go with this guy, even though she only just met him and he will likely expect something in return. She's had experience dodging the fumblings of horny guys. She is seventeen, after all. It's not like she's never been kissed. She can handle this guy, too.

"Okay, thanks. I accept your offer of a ride. When do we leave?"

"First thing in the morning. You can stay with me tonight." He attacks the second cheeseburger. "You shouldn't of took them boots off," he says, while still chewing. "You'll never git 'em back on. I'll hafta carry you."

Lindy snorts, picks up her boots, then gets to her feet and starts away, saying, "See you tomorrow."

"Don't be late." he calls after her. "I'll be pullin' out by eight."

She gives a little wave and strides off down the dimly-lit pathway, avoiding the detritus of a carnival crowd and puddles left over from the earlier rainstorm as much as possible. At least her feet are cooling off.

Not for the first time that day, she curses herself for an idiot. One, for buying the god-awful cowboy boots too small. As if half a size is going to make enough of a difference to make her feet look small and cute like Jillian's. Two, for throwing the running shoes away. At the time it made sense not to lug them around, dangling from their laces, making her look like an idiot. Now, she'd give anything to have them back.

Can she walk all the way home in stocking feet?

NICK WATCHES HER WALK away, back ramrod straight, limping when she steps on something that hurts. One of the cowboys at the next table asks, "Strike out, Painless?"

One of the others asks, "Now who you gonna be pullin' out of by eight?" He makes an obscene pumping gesture with his fist and they all laugh.

"Didn't git enough action tonight, Painless?" one of the others asks.

"Too bad he don't care about his buddies. Held us up so long by the time we got here, the girls already left."

"Yeah. Thanks for nuthin', Painless."

"None of you losers would git anywhere with those girls unless there was no one else in the place anyway," Nick says. "You seen who they left with."

He's quiet for a moment, then lifts his chin in Lindy's direction and adds, "She'll be lucky if she don't step on glass or somethin' 'n' git her feet cut."

The big cowboy at the next table nods toward the carnies congregating under the bluish mercury vapor light where the midway starts, and says: "She'll be goddamn lucky if a cut foot's all she gits." He stands abruptly, his chair scraping back and almost tipping as he does. He watches intently as Lindy approaches the group of men. "I don't like it. We should go sort them greasy bastards out."

"Goddamn it, Gorgeous, sit down." one of the others hisses. "I mean it. If she's dumb enough to walk into that. Well, if they grab her up, that's different. If not, stay the hell outta it. You git into it, then we all end up in it."

"Them weedy little bastards is already shitfaced. We'd make short work of them."

"That's what you think. Them weedy little bastards is tough. Besides, they don't play by the rules 'n' I fer one don't need my belly slit."

As they watch, Lindy nears the men under the light, and slows. They're passing around a bottle. Some are drunkenly unsteady on their feet. When one goes a few steps away and urinates on an overflowing garbage can right in front of her, she stops.

He looks up and calls out, "Hey, beautiful. Wanna give me a hand?" His buddies hoot and whistle.

After a beat, Lindy turns and picks her way back to the cantina. She nods to the big cowboy standing at the table next to the one she'd just vacated and slips into the chair next to Nick.

"Oh, yer back," Nick says. The corners of his eyes crinkle and he gives her a wink. "You fergit somethin'?"

"Maybe I could sleep in your car?" she asks.

"Oh, sure, you can sleep with me," he says, loud enough so his friends don't miss it. Then, more quietly, "It's a truck 'n' camper. There's my bunk 'n' the table makes into a bed. Room fer both of us. I swear, I'll be a perfect gennelman." He picks up the last bits of potato and wipes up the ketchup with them before sticking them in his mouth. He gives his fingers a lick before wiping them on a napkin. "But if it makes you feel better," he continues, "I'll take the truck."

"No, I'll take the truck." Lindy says. "But do you have an extra blanket I could borrow?"

"Sure."

Who is she, really? Nick wonders, searching her face for a clue. He doesn't remember seeing her around. No buckle bunny would wear that crappy touristy hat and dude boots. Or have to be introduced to the winning-est cowboy at the Stampede. She looked lost and worried; the air of relief that came over her when he told her she could sleep in his rig might have been comical if it wasn't so pitiful. *She's just a kid*, he thinks, *a lost, vulnerable kid, putting on a brave face.*

But he must be reading her wrong. She must want a good time or she wouldn't be looking for a cowboy at this time of night.

FOUR

Calgary, Alberta

Monday, July 19, 1976

When it comes down to it, Nick refuses to let Lindy sleep in the truck, and since she won't sleep in the second bed in the camper despite his assurances he'll stay in his own bunk, he spends the night in the cab.

It's dawn and Lindy is starting to come awake when there's a knock on the door and she hears Nick on the other side saying, "Rise and shine. Can I come in?"

She sits up, swinging her bare legs to dangle over the edge of the bunk, wishing for about the fifteenth time that she had pyjamas instead of the skimpy baby dolls and cursing herself as an idiot for not sleeping in her clothes. She gathers the blanket around her shoulders and says, "Okay."

Coffee and bacon smells come in the door with Nick and he sets takeout from the cantina on the table. "World famous bacon, egg and sausage breakfast burgers," he says as he slides onto the bench at the table.

"Thank you," she says, clutching the blanket tight around herself. "I'll pay you back ..."

"Naww, my treat. I always have two but I only got one for you. Will that be enough? Come sit." He smiles and pushes the paper cup of coffee to the opposite side of the table. He's attacking his sandwich and doesn't look up at her again until he stops chewing and takes a sip of coffee. "Ain't you coming down from there?"

She shakes her head.

"Oh. Yer naked."

"I am not."

"Yer not? Just want to sit there? Okay, well, I guess you can eat where you are." He slides out from behind the table, picks up the sandwich, and takes the two steps to stand close and hand it to her. "Nice legs."

"Umm, thanks." She gathers the blanket tighter, tugging it over her knees. The sandwich in the little bag, with its thick sausage patty, bacon sticking out, the frill of a fried egg showing, is oozing sauce and the fillings are already starting to slide out of the bun. Eating it one-handed won't be easy. The aroma of the sandwich makes her salivary glands react so powerfully she has to swallow a couple of times; her stomach growls, but if she lets go of the blanket to take the sandwich in both hands, the blanket will almost certainly slide off and she'll be sitting in her baby dolls. Even underwear would be better—at least her bra and panties aren't see-through. To make matters worse, he's watching closely, standing close enough she can hear him breathing and smell his coffee breath, wearing an amused grin. She feels heat rising to her face when she realizes he knows she's embarrassed, and he's enjoying it.

Maybe falling in with Nick wasn't such a good idea. Who knows what he's capable of? He was nothing if not gentlemanly last night, but what might he do in the coming week, when they're alone together? What if he takes her miles from civilization? Maybe she should go home after all. If she can get her boots on this morning, she can walk home. Even in bare feet, for that matter. It's daylight now, and it'll only take a few hours. Her mother will have a fit, but that's nothing new. The problem will be getting away again next weekend, and somehow getting to High Prairie.

As if reading her thoughts, Nick says, "Here." Taking the sandwich from her hand, he puts it on the table, picks up his coffee and sandwich, then takes the two steps to the door, saying, "I'll wait outside until you git dressed." He opens the door, hops to the ground, and bumps the door shut behind him.

She scurries down off the bunk. As she's dressing, it comes to her that he did the honorable thing. She shouldn't be surprised. But she is. Pleasantly.

She's relieved to find she can get her boots on this morning. She stuffs the baby dolls into her purse and fastens her hair into a ponytail before sliding behind the table and calling out, "Okay."

Nick climbs in, sits across from her, and pulls his second sandwich and all the condiments out of the paper sack.

"I take my coffee black but I never asked how you take yers, so I got cream 'n' sugar, just in case," he says, pushing a couple of creamers and little packets of sugar across the table to her. "Hope it's enough."

Drinking coffee seems to be such a grown-up pleasure she doesn't want to admit she doesn't like it. That is, except for her mother's, which has enough Bailey's in it you can barely even taste the coffee. She adds cream and keeps adding sugar until the little packets are used up. It's drinkable. The sandwich, though, is so good she forgets about the dirty kitchen it came from.

"So," Nick says as he chews, "what do you think? The sandwich as good as advertised?"

"Mmmm," she says, savoring her mouthful and swallowing before answering, "Really good. Really, really good"

"Well, it should take us over until lunch, anyway."

"How long will it take us to get to High Prairie?"

"Well, we're not going straight there. Before we leave town, I need to hit a Safeway store 'n' lay in food for the week. And of course, the liquor board store. We'll meet up with the others later today 'n' go the rest of the way together."

"Oh. Okay. Can we stop by a bank?"

"Sure. I got bankin' to do, too."

"Perfect." She sips the rapidly-cooling coffee, then asks, "What others?"

"You remember those guys I was with when you met me last night? The four of us are travelling together. Melon knows a place about halfway to High Prairie that's open range. In the foothills. A nice spot to spend a few days."

"Oh. Open range? So, no toilets or showers?" She feels a niggling worry. That's away from civilization, for sure, although there will be others there too. Just men? Who knows what kind of people they are?

"Where'd you think we'd be spendin' the week?"

"I didn't think about it, I guess." She pushes her doubts to the back of her mind and takes a bite of her sandwich, considering the question as she chews. "I guess I just thought we'd go to High Prairie and I could get a motel room and wait for, um, Mr. Larsen there."

"You got the moolah to spend a week in a motel room? What kind of job do you have, anyway?"

"I, er, haven't got a job this summer yet. I'm a student."

"Oh. Well, you don't want to be spending yer summer job money on a motel. *Mister* Larsen won't show up until the weekend anyway. Camping out on the range is nice, better than a campground, plus it's a nice break for the horses, and we don't have to pay for stalls or a campsite. You can stay with me and save yer money. Besides, I think you'll like it. You ever camped anywhere but a campground?"

"No. Never camped anywhere, actually. Unless you count the backyard when I was about eight. Or summer camp. But of course then, we had bunkhouses."

"Never went on vacation?"

"Sure, just—you know, flew wherever we were going and stayed in a hotel."

"Oh yeah? Where'd you fly to?"

"Umm, well, Hawaii a few times. Disneyland. Italy once."

"Ahhh. I see. Yer a princess."

Princess? The way he said it seems like an insult. Lindy feels herself blushing and blurts out, "A little out of your league?" As soon as the words leave her mouth, she regrets it. That was definitely an insult, uncalled for, and she's relying on him so it's foolish to antagonize him.

But if he's offended, he doesn't show it. He chuckles and stuffs half his second sandwich into his mouth.

Airdrie, Alberta

Monday, July 19, 1976

NICK AND LINDY ARE the first of the group to arrive at the agreed meeting place, the Husky truck stop in Airdrie. Nick unloads his horse and leads him to the wide grassy area next to the pumps where there are picnic tables, then sits on one, holding the lead rope while the horse grazes. He pulls a wad of bills out of his pocket, peels off a twenty, and holds it out. "Go git us some lunch, okay? They make decent burgers here."

"My treat. You bought breakfast," Lindy says, feeling flush after a stop at the bank.

"Oh, yer a modern princess? Everything's Dutch?"

"Er, I'm not an *anything* princess." She gives him what she hopes is a severe frown before continuing, "I wonder if they have salads on the take-out menu. You want one if they do?"

"If you git it with onions, lettuce 'n' tomato, there's enough salad on the burger. And onion rings. I like onion rings. That's vegetables. You can have a salad, but we won't be eating supper fer a while so you might want somethin' more substantial. Git some snacks for the ride, too. *Princess.*"

"Quit calling me that. People will think it's, like—well, they'll think we're a couple."

"Okay, Princess,"—he grins and winks—"but I'll tell you what, goin' Dutch ain't how it works in my world." He presses the twenty into her hand.

After a moment's indecision, Lindy says, "Okay," and heads to the restaurant.

It's after one when the first two rigs arrive and pull up to the pumps. The drivers get out and acknowledge Nick with a wave. Just minutes later, the fourth and last rig turns off the highway and pulls up to the pumps. A cowboy with the biggest moustache Lindy has ever seen climbs out from behind the wheel, speaks to the attendant, and then comes to join the group forming on the lawn.

"Sorry I'm late, folks," he says.

"You ain't late," Nick tells him, "or at least if you were, these guys were too. We been here nearly a couple hours already. What the hell kept you guys?"

"We stopped fer lunch," the big cowboy with the flat nose says.

"I had to make a side trip to pick up a passenger," the latest arrival explains, and indicates the small dark-haired woman heading toward them from the other side of his rig.

"Red." the men shout almost in unison.

"Didn't know you was joinin' us," the short cowboy calls out. "My stars, how'd we git so lucky?"

She smiles and gives a little wave as she comes to join the group on the grassy area and gives Petey a scratch. Once they all greet Red, Nick loops an arm around Lindy and says, "Hey, everyone, this is Princess."

"Nick." She gives him a black look and shrugs his arm off her shoulders as she feels the blood rushing to her face. "My name's Lindy," she tells the group.

"Hi, Lindy," the cowboy with the walrus moustache says. "Princess ain't such a bad handle, compared to some. They call me Melon. I got no goddamn idea why."

"Like watermelon. Because his head's so big, in every sense of the word." This from the small, slightly-built cowboy. "I'm Reggie but everyone calls me Wiggles, 'n' I know why. It's because I can't stand sittin' around on my ass for hours like the rest of these lazy bastards. And my lady here is Red," he says, indicating the woman. Her hair is dark with threads of grey. Her skin is deeply tanned and there isn't a redhead freckle to be seen.

"Hi, Lindy," she says, "And I ain't his lady, if you want to know."

"No she ain't," Melon says, "she's everyone's lady."

"That don't sound good. What he means is, we all think of her as a lady." Wiggles starts singing "She's a lady. La la la. She's a lay—dee."

"Tom Jones you ain't," Red tells him, "but thanks."

The last one to be introduced is Gorgeous, who, with his smooth brown skin, dark brown eyes and hair so black it's nearly blue really is gorgeous, or at least handsome, but for his flattened nose. He towers over Wiggles and Red, and is taller than Nick and Melon, too. "No need to explain why they call me Gorgeous," he says, taking Lindy's hand and giving it a squeeze, "these homely bastards are jealous."

"Yeah, we all wish we had noses that were beat to crap," Nick says.

"It can be arranged," Gorgeous says, "although in yer case, Painless, it'd take some real work. Not that I'd mind doin' it fer yuh."

"Er, umm, what happened to your nose, Gorgeous?" Lindy asks.

"Ahh, shit, Lindy," Melon says, "it took more'n once to git it like that. Don't go feelin' sorry fer him. He likes to fight 'n' gits his nose broke damn near every time."

When the rigs are all gassed up and bugs cleaned off the windshields, and everyone's used the washrooms, Petey is loaded into the trailer and the convoy heads out, northbound on Highway #2.

FIVE

Jackpot Rodeo School

Rocky Mountain House, Alberta

Monday, July 19, 1976

The farrier is working on one of the school horses. Cam holds the mare's lead rope, although she's standing so patiently while the work's being done he almost doesn't need to. Diamond stands nearby waiting his turn. His lead rope is looped over the rail and he's favouring one hind foot; his eyes are closed, and his lower lip droops as he naps in the sun.

The farrier straightens and he says, "Okay, you can put her back out." He pulls a pack of cigarettes out of his shirt pocket and lights one, drawing deep as Cam leads the mare toward the far pasture gate.

When he returns, Cam leads Diamond to the forge. The farrier sticks his half-smoked cigarette in the corner of his mouth; smoke curls up causing him to squint one eye as he bends and picks up Diamond's near front foot. He scrapes away at it with the hoof pick for a moment, then clucks his tongue and lets the horse put his foot down. "Can't put them shoes back on," he says as he straightens, "they're wore out."

"Come on, Jake. They got a few more miles in 'em."

"I ain't resettin' them. They're too small fer starters. Lousy keg shoes. If you want 'em reset, yer gonna hafta do it yerself. Looks like that wouldn't be the first time. You can't make the hoof fit the shoe,

43

Gobbler. No wonder he's ouchy half the time. With them contracted heels he'd be better off barefoot. Should pull 'em off 'n' then turn him out somewhere, because he'd prob'ly be ouchy full time fer a while 'n' you'd need a different horse for the rest of the season. How old did you say he is? You're gonna need another horse pretty quick anyhow."

"I made a lot of money on this horse. He's been a little off lately but he's still better'n half the horses on the tour. I ain't gittin another horse."

"Okay, then." Jake takes a final deep drag on his smoke, then drops it and crushes it under his boot. "Tell you what. You can owe me until payday if you ain't got the wherewithal."

"I got the money," Cam says, scowling. "Course I got the money. What makes you think I ain't got the money? I don't want to spend it this week, is all. I got travelin' expenses coming up this weekend. Goin' to Helena."

"Oh yeah? Why? Thought Porky said High Prairie."

"Porky's determined to go to High Prairie; he's chasin' after a piece of ass, no other reason, or he wouldn't be going to that rinky-dink show when there's big money in Helena. I'm goin' south. Besides the purse, there's better stock, better chance of gettin' a high score. Which I need right now. Makin' up fer some mizzable rides in Calgary."

"Well, I doubt your horse gives a shit what you need the money fer. He's been wearin' these too long already 'n' they were the shits to start with."

"Ay-yuh, I already *deduced* that from what you said before."

Jake stands arms akimbo, looks off across the yard for a minute, and then blows out a breath. "Well, look. I hate to see a good horse ruined by bad shoein'. I'll give him some decent shoes to git started remedyin' them contracted heels. But you owe me."

"Done."

Jake selects nippers from his tool bucket and sets to work pulling Diamond's shoes.

After a bit, Cam asks, "Any you boys like a friendly game of stud?"

"Yup, you betcha. Usually a pretty good game on a pay Friday. Yer welcome to sit in. Five dollar buy-in 'n' two buck ante."

"Oh yeah? How many guys, usually?"

"Ten. Twelve. Sometimes more."

"In the bunkhouse?

"Nope, down in the classroom. It's Frank's game. All hush-hush. Boss's wife got some crazy religion; if she finds out about it she'll go on a rampage 'n' make him shut 'er down so we gotta keep it on the Q.T."

"What time?"

"Usually get set up by eight. If there's enough guys hangin' around earlier, there's likely to be a game of Stook goin' before that."

"Stook, eh?"

"Stook. And bring yer own libations."

Cam says nothing while Jake selects shoes, puts them into the forge, and sets to work trimming Diamond's hooves. Finally, he says, "Might win Diamond's shoes off you."

"You better have more'n just Diamond's shoes to play for."

Cam rubs Diamond's forehead and grins. "Friday's payday, ain't it?"

SIX

Rocky Mountain Foothills

Monday, July 19, 1976

The scenery north of Calgary is pleasant: gentle hills dotted with low shrubs and sloughs. Lindy's seldom been out of the city except on a plane, and is enjoying it. Every slough seems to be teeming with ducks and other waterfowl. Seas of crops wave in the wind and endless pastures are home to herds of cattle and horses. Nick points out different cattle breeds: a herd of black ones he calls Angus. The reddy-brown cattle with white heads are Herefords. A group of white cattle he calls Charolais and says they're a new, imported French breed.

Highway 2 is four lanes divided by a wide grassy swale, seventy miles per hour speed limit, so the little convoy makes good time, at least until they turn west and head deeper into the foothills. Despite the slow going on the winding gravel road, they come to the chosen spot in the late afternoon.

There's a small herd of cattle already bedded down there. Wiggles and Melon get their lariats and begin swinging them around and whistling, encouraging the herd to move on. There's one tense moment when a big steer bellows and turns back toward Wiggles as if to challenge him, but when the rest of the cattle go crashing through the low brush and across the creek, he thinks better of it and charges after them.

With the cattle gone, camper-horse trailer rigs settle in, forming a large square. That done, the first order is to unload the horses. Nick drops the ramp on his trailer, unhooks the butt chain, and goes in beside his horse to back him out.

"I'm going to take Petey down to the creek so he can have a drink before I stake him out," he says to Lindy. "You come and stand in the creek."

"What? Stand in the creek? Why?"

"Yer boots are still uncomfortable, ain't they?"

"Well, yeah."

"So, stand in the water there until they're good and soaked. Then leave 'em on until they dry. Tomorrow, they'll be broke in."

They follow the others down a shallow bank to what appears to be a well-used watering hole, no doubt the reason the cattle chose this spot. Lindy hesitates. It seems like a crazy thing to do to nice leather boots, but if it works like Nick says it will, worth it. She wades in and stands in ankle-deep water.

"You better not be fooling about this," she says. Nick's grin does nothing to assure her he's not.

Petey comes splashing in beside her and starts pawing. "Hey!" she shouts, and jumps away.

Nick laughs and says, "Sorry. He does like to do that. I forgot."

When Petey quits pawing, drops his head and starts drinking, Lindy moves up beside him, stroking his silky shoulder and finger-combing the short mane on his withers. Watching him, seeing the way his ears flick back and forth with each swallow, the feel of his warm skin under her fingers and the gurgling of the water as it slides by is peaceful. She looks back over her shoulder at Nick, who is watching her. He grins and says, "Nice view from up here."

Standing in the dappled shade holding the lead rope, one hand on his hip, he looks relaxed and confident. The giant silver buckle on the belt that hugs his narrow hips flashes when a stray sunbeam finds it. Just visible in the shade of his hat brim, his eyes twinkle. His grin is infectious. She thinks, *nice view from down here, too,* and smiles back.

When Petey has finished drinking, Nick leads him back to the open ground near his trailer and hands the rope to Lindy. "Let him graze, just watch he doesn't step on the rope," he cautions. "I'll get the peg and chain."

All four horses are staked out and settled for the night. The dry cow pies are stacked at the edge of the campsite, saved in case they want to hold a cow-pie-throwing contest sometime. Gorgeous has a shovel and is cleaning up the wet ones. He good-naturedly shrugs off Melon's comment that he's finally found a job he's suited for.

The men haul rocks from the creek bed to make a fire pit and gather dead wood and cut willow wands for wiener roasting from the stand of aspens and scrub bushes next to the creek. Camp chairs are brought out and placed around the fire pit. Melon produces a folding table and sets it up next to his camper. Red gets out a five gallon pail from the back of Melon's truck.

"What's that for?" Lindy asks.

"Our biffy. Come on. I'll show you," Red replies, and leads the way into the bush. When they reach a good-size aspen fairly near the creek, Red puts the can at the base and squirms it around until it's not wobbly.

"So this is where we go to, um,"

"Yeah. The guys can easily pee anywhere so this is just fer their big jobs, but we can use it whenever. You okay with that?"

Lindy shrugs and says, "I guess I'll have to be."

"You'll get used to it," Red assures her.

When they're back at camp, the two of them make stacks of baloney sandwiches, open cans of beans, and that, together with beers, is their evening meal.

"Tomorrow I'll be organized 'n' the grub'll be better," Red promises as everyone helps themselves.

"I like baloney sandwiches," Gorgeous says. "Could use a little Dee John mustard, though."

"What the hell're you talkin' about, Dee John mustard?" Melon asks.

"You know, that spicy stuff they put on them Montreal Smoked Meat sandwiches. Ain't you seen 'em? They had 'em on the midway this year."

"I swear, some people will even complain about a classic like a baloney sandwich." Red says. "What's the world comin' to?"

Wiggles says, "You notice the lack of the Dee John mustard ain't slowin' him down."

"Gorgeous would eat shit on a stick," Melon says. He gives Red a one-armed hug as she spoons beans onto his plate.

"Only if it has Dee John mustard on it," Gorgeous says with a grins as he takes another sandwich from Red and says, "Thank you, darlin'."

Having no camp chairs, Nick and Lindy take their plates and sit on a hay bale near his truck.

"Didn't know baloney sandwiches and beans could taste so good," Lindy comments.

"Everything tastes better out here."

After a bit, Lindy looks up just as Gorgeous takes the last of the beans and hugs Red for it. She asks quietly, "Is Gorgeous Red's boyfriend? I thought Melon said she was, umm, *everyone's*."

"You took that wrong. Don't know if she's with Gorgeous. He has a couple of lady friends here 'n' there, don't think she's one of them. But neither of 'em's married so they can do what they want. Same goes fer her 'n' Wiggles. Melon's the only one of us that's married. If she wants to get it on with him 'n' he's into it, too, I don't care about that, neither," he answers, mopping the last of his beans off his paper plate with his sandwich. "She never slept with me. Other than that, it's none of my business." His tone is mild but his expression is stern.

He abruptly gets to his feet and turns away, taking his plate to toss it in the fire pit. He comes back to his truck, walking past her without a glance or a word, to dig a plastic steer's head and a flat, round metal can out from behind the seat. He sticks the head on one end of the bale next to her, then opens the rope can and pulls out a lariat. Fussing with it for a bit, he shakes out a loop, and gives it a couple of swings over his head. "Excuse me, ma'am."

Lindy jumps to her feet and stands next to the truck to finish her beans, then takes her plate to the firepit. When she comes back, she leans against the fender of his truck to watch as Nick makes repeated throws at the dummy. The loop usually goes over the head, but when he looks up at her for a moment just as he throws, the loop skitters off to the side.

"Damn," he mutters under his breath and coils the rope for another try.

He looks at Lindy again and says, "Lindy, I don't think she sleeps with any of 'em. She's sweet on Porky, who as you know, ain't here. She's always first up, gets coffee on, starts up the griddle. Says she cooks as good as she looks 'n' she sure knows her way around a camp stove. The grub's guaranteed to be better with her here, plus she's a real nice person. We like havin' her along. Nuthin' more to it than that." He clicks his tongue and turns his attention back to his rope.

Building a larger loop he swings it over his head, then drops it neatly over Lindy, who lets out a squeak. He shortens his end of the rope as he walks toward her, tightening the loop and pulling her off balance. He puts his arms around her as if to steady her, and says, "Gotcha."

"Ow," she squawks, rubbing her shoulder.

"Did the rope scuff your arm? Sorry. Here, I'll kiss it better." Before she can decline, he has her arm and makes a show of laying smacking kisses from her wrist to her elbow. She draws in a quick breath as his warm masculine scent, a blend of horse and sweat and aftershave, wafts up around her.

Then he straightens and lifts his loop off over her head. The big grin is back as he steps away and coils the rope for another throw at the dummy.

Lindy isn't sure he's genuinely sorry, but the rope didn't really hurt all that much, and at least his frown is gone. If he was annoyed because she asked about Red's relationship to the men in this group, he's forgiven her.

She's been thinking about the night before, that hand with the wedding ring cupping Carla's breast. Carla wore no rings. She realizes that cowboy wass married, just not to Carla. If he's her boyfriend, obviously neither of them cares. Suddenly, she's blasted with the memory again, but this time, it's her mother instead of Carla leaving with the cowboy. She can't make out the cowboy's face but knows it's her father.

From time to time over the years since she learned where babies come from, she has wondered how it was with her biological parents. She blamed her mother, not understanding how she could have let it happen. She thinks, *she's got some nerve, always on my case, wanting to know where I go and what I do, all suspicious. Sure, I did stuff with Jerry, and now Glen, but I know where to draw the line.*

And then just as suddenly, she understands. *She thinks I'm like her.* And these men are so masculine. No pasty-white, sweating Hal DeWitts in three-piece suits but real men. Once Marie fell in with guys like this, maybe it was inevitable.

She watches the handsome cowboy fooling around with his lariat. He's the type of guy she's always detested: the show-off sniggering at the back of the class; hanging around the parking lot smoking and making suggestive remarks to all the girls as they go by; swaggering through the school as if he's god's gift. Nick's got that cocky grin. That bounce in his step. But the stirring she felt when he put his arms around her and said *gotcha*. If the others weren't watching... If they were alone... Although they barely know each other, she would have let him kiss her.

She might even have wanted more than one kiss.

RED IS BUSY OUTSIDE Melon's rig. She starts a pot of coffee on the Coleman gas stove. Hunching over bags and boxes on the ground, she organizes the food everyone contributed to the stash according to what has to go in the fridge in Melon's camper, and what can be left in the coolers or in bags.

Melon and Wiggles, holding beers, join her and hand her one. She straightens and takes the beer, and they all stand looking across the campsite pretending not to watch Nick and Lindy.

Lindy is sitting cross-legged on the ground with her book open, reading, or at least trying to. He's quit fooling with the rope and is now sitting on the bale that Lindy is leaning back against. He plucks a long piece of grass and lightly touches her ear. She swats, as if at a bug. He does it again. Lindy swats but keeps reading.

He moves on to her neck below her ear. This time when she swats, she catches the grass, turns her head and frowns at Nick. He barks a laugh, and when she gets to her knees and faces him, giving him a playful shove, he does an exaggerated roll backward off the bale, pulling her with him. She lands on top of him, squeaks in protest, and scrambles to her feet.

"Aww, ain't that cute," Wiggles says with a sigh.

"Cute? Good Christ, Wiggles, yer such an old woman." Melon works a toothpick through his moustache into his mouth. "Why's she still with him? Why the hell didn't he turf her out this morning? This ain't like him."

"He must-a liked her enough to want to git to know her better."

"Pffft." Melon huffs. "Or she's good enough he wants more. Still. How long d'you think before he dumps her? Ten bucks says she don't last past High Prairie."

"I'll take that," Wiggles says.

"Okay. How about this: if he dumps her any time before Strathmore, I win. If she lasts past Strathmore, you win."

"That's not what you said. You said High Prairie 'n' now you wanna add two more rodeos? If she lasts past Medicine Hat I win, 'n' that's worth more'n ten. Make it twenty."

"You're on."

"She ain't like the others. He won't dump her, least not fer a while," Wiggles opines. "She's pretty 'n' she seems nice enough. I say, good fer him."

"I know you guys would bet on anything," Red says, "but I don't like you bettin' on Nick like that. It ain't nice. It's his life 'n' yer gonna jinx it. You, I trust, but Melon ain't above doin' something to mess it up just to make sure he gits yer twenty bucks."

"You got me all wrong, Red," Melon grumbles.

"I doubt it. Yer all three the same, anything fer a joke. I'll be watchin' you guys. I'm worried, though. She's pretty 'n' maybe she's nice, too," Red agrees, "but you remember how it was with Jennifer. Painless is all bluff 'n' tough talk, fun 'n' games, but when he fell for Jennifer, he fell hard 'n' quick. And I'd say, goin' by how he looks at this one, after just one day? Callin' her Princess? I just hope the hell she ain't another Jennifer."

"Well, she's no buckle bunny, so that's a good start." Wiggles says.

"No, she ain't now, goin' by her touristy get-up, but she did bunk in with him after knowin' him no more'n a few minutes even though she was lookin' fer Gobbler." Melon points out. "They all gotta start somewhere. Maybe she wants to start with champions, even if they're has-beens. Wouldn't be the first gal to give ol' Gobbler a toss just to say they did. Painless is a big boy 'n' by now. I guess he's learnt if she'll sleep with him first jump outta the gate, she'll do the same with the next cowboy."

"Not always," Wiggles says, "Jennifer stuck with him a while."

"Yeah, long enough to make him think it could come to somethin'," Red says. "And I wouldn't sell Gobbler short if I was you, Melon. He's still a good-lookin' guy 'n' he ain't always an assmeat, although I'll wager he's a lot nicer to pretty girls than to you old buggers."

"I'll grant you that," Wiggles says, "we all seen him in action. He can be a charmer. At least up until he's got a skin full."

They're quiet for a bit, then Red exclaims, "Holy shit. I think I know who she is."

"Say, what?" Gorgeous is just coming around the back of the camper with the jugs of water he fetched from the creek. He sets them on the table and comes to stand next to Red.

"Red thinks she knows who that Lindy gal is," Melon tells him.

"She ain't lookin' to knock boots with Gobbler, 'n' she ain't preggers or lookin' to make trouble fer him like one of you assmeats suggested, neither," Red continues, "she's lookin' fer him 'cause she's his daughter."

"Seriously?" Melon says. "What makes you think that?"

"Ain't you seen that picture he shows around?"

"I have," Gorgeous says, "but I thought he was makin' shit up, as usual. Thought it was one of them pitchers in the pitcher frames they sell at Woolworth's."

"That where you got yer fam'ly album from, Gorgeous?" Melon asks.

"Gorgeous," Wiggles says, "you landed on yer head too many times. If it was one of them, it would have words printed on it. Sometimes yer as thick as fourteen wooden shithouse seats."

"Don't you guys remember that cute li'l dark-haired gal that was with him, oh, maybe about twenty years ago now? What the heck was her name? Hmmm." Red pulls the elastic out of her ponytail and scratches the back of her head. "Was with him a year, maybe longer. I know she was with him a couple of Stampedes, anyway. Then she was gone. Gobbler never said what happened. You guys don't remember?"

"Way before my time," Melon says.

"Well, thanks a whole helluva lot for remindin' me how old I am," Red says. "Yer older than me, Wiggles. You must remember."

"Aw, sweet Red," Wiggles sighs, "I'm older'n you but I wasn't rodeoin' back then. My wife wouldn't let me. I just got into it when she passed."

"That's why you started late? Always wondered. Sorry, Reggie."

"It was a long time ago, but thanks, Red. 'N' don't worry, you'll always be young 'n' beautiful to me. I'm writing a song about you. I call it Red Rose of Avonlea." He sings, "*Sweet Red Rose of Avonlea, I love her, but she don't love me. I love her so, can't let her know, 'cause her heart belongs to Porkeeee. Sweet Red Rose of Avonlea.*"

"Fer Christ's sake Wiggles." Melon exclaims, shaking his head. "That's really shitty."

"I guess you could do better, Melon? I know it still needs some work. It ain't finished yet."

"You really think Porky is a good name to have in a love song?" Melon asks.

"I didn't know you was from Avonlea, Red," Gorgeous says. "Do you know Ernie Stair?"

"I'm from Maple Creek, not Avonlea."

"How could it be Sweet Red Rose of Maple Creek? Think about it. It would help if I knew yer name, too, Red," Wiggles suggests.

"It'd be more helpful if you didn't try to make it fit the tune of Barbara Allen. But trust me, it wouldn't be no easier with my real name 'n' no one in their right mind would wanna make a song outa it, that's fer sure." Red shakes her head, but gives Wiggles a fond grin before continuing. "I could be wrong. Don't say nuthin'. If she *is* Cam's daughter, she must have her reasons fer keepin' it to herself. Everyone's entitled to secrets." She scratches her head again, puts her beer down next to the camp stove and draws her hair back into the elastic. "You sure they didn't know each other before? Like from university or something?"

"Yup." Melon pulls the toothpick out of the moustache that completely covers his lips. "Met fer the first time at the cantina last night."

"So they can't possibly just be friends, then."

"I'd say no," Wiggles contributes, "or he'd of said so, where he knew her from 'n' so on. He didn't call her his friend, did he? He said something like, *this is Princess*, not *this is my friend Princess*. Anyway, you seen him teasin' her. You talk about how he looks at her? Well, she may be playin' hard to git, but she's lookin' back."

"Yeah, that's what worries me," Red sighs. "As we all know, Gobbler ain't sensible when it comes to Painless."

"No he ain't, even at the best of times," Melon says, shaking his head slowly. "If she really is his daughter, I dunno which he'd hate more, her bein' one of the tour gals, or her not bein' one 'n' Painless takin' advantage of her."

WIGGLES, MELON, AND Red are in chairs around the campfire. Gorgeous is cross-legged on the ground next to Red. Nick comes from the tack storage area at the front of his trailer carrying a thick rectangular cushion. He checks to see which direction the smoke is blowing before placing it on the ground near the fire. He looks at Lindy with a grin and says, "Have a seat, Princess."

"Thanks," Lindy tells him, and sinks onto the cushion.

Nick pulls a two bottles of beer out of a cooler, opens one, and hands it to Lindy.

"Thanks again," she says.

He pops the lid off the other bottle, then drops down beside her.

"Hey."

"What?"

"Get your own cushion."

"This is the only one I got 'n' it ain't even a cushion. It's Petey's saddle pad. Can't you smell it?" He slips his arm around her shoulders. She shrugs it off but he just grins and takes her hand instead. She pulls it away and he takes it again.

"Stop it." she hisses under her breath. He brings her hand to his lips and kisses her knuckles before dropping it.

Gorgeous gets up and goes to his camper, coming back with marshmallows. He spears them on a willow wand and toasts marshmallows for everyone while Wiggles strums his guitar and starts a long, drawn out rendition of *Ghost Riders in the Sky*. Drawn out, because everyone chimes in at the top of their lungs, on the "Yippee aye yay. Yippee aye yo-o-oh." chorus.

They request the tune several times, and everyone laughs when they're quiet and can hear coyotes in the near distance, howling as if singing along.

"I've only ever heard that in the movies," Lindy whispers. There's a catch in her voice. "It's so beautiful."

"Aww, Princess, don't cry."

"I'm not crying, silly," Lindy sniffs, "but it *is* beautiful. And quit calling me Princess."

"Okay," he says, and puts his arm around her, pulling her in tight against him. This time she doesn't squirm free, telling herself it's okay because the evening is getting chilly. She would let Glen put his arm around her, and they're just friends. Well, although she'd never admit it to her mother, they're very friendly friends, even though she finds him only mildly attractive. Necking with him is more experimentation than lust, so it's easy to call a halt to it no matter how worked up he gets. Even in the thick of things, he doesn't make her blood race like just being close to Nick does. It's a strange, foreign, pleasant feeling. She takes a deep breath and relaxes into his embrace.

Before long, people start yawning and stretching, getting up and saying good night. The fire is stirred and the remains of coffee dumped on it.

"If you gals want to use the head in my rig, yer welcome to," Melon says.

"Oh, great." Lindy says. It was bad enough going into the bush to squat over the bucket bare-assed during daylight; the idea of pushing through the low bushes and into the trees to find the bucket and dropping her pants in the dark when you couldn't see a bear or cougar if it was three feet away is almost petrifying.

"That's a good offer, Mel," Red says, "but we're fine." She turns to Lindy and tells her, "We don't have to go all the way to the can, if that's what yer worried about," she tells Lindy. They go away from the light of the campfire and out of sight behind the campers while the guys pee into the firepit.

From where they're squatting, Lindy and Red hear the men hooting. "What do they find to talk about while they're peeing, anyway?" Lindy wonders, as she stands and straightens her clothes.

"I don't need to hear the words to guess what they're saying. You know men; it'll be something to do with who can pee the furthest, or the most, or maybe they're just comparing the size of their dicks."

"Seriously?" Lindy giggles.

"Yup," Red says, "men. They may look like adults, but they never really grow up."

Back in camp, they say good-night and Lindy goes to Nick's camper. He's waiting by the open door. She climbs in and he closes it behind her. This morning, they agreed it was silly for either of them to spend an uncomfortable night in the truck when there were two good beds in the camper, and once parked, he made the table into a bed.

She squirms out of her clothes, folding everything carefully so her underwear is out of sight, and gets into the Baby Dolls, once again cursing under her breath for being stupid enough to choose them simply because of their packability. She would have been better off to leave the book. Would she want her father to see her in the skimpy sheer things the first night they met? But then, she wasn't expecting to be sleeping in a camper. She expected a proper motel room, with guest robes in the closet. He's a champion. He'd have better accommodations than a camper with no fridge or toilet. Wouldn't he?

Once she climbs under the covers and turns so she's facing the wall, she calls out, "Okay."

The door squeaks open and the fold-out steps creak under his weight as Nick climbs inside and pulls the door shut behind him.

She hears soft noises of snaps, zippers, and cloth rustling as he strips, dropping his clothes where he stands. "There goes my gaunch," he says.

Lindy squirms and pulls the covers up over her head.

"Not interested?"

"No."

He lets out a huge theatrical sigh and vaults into his bunk. There's a stir of blankets being shuffled about, then quiet.

"Good night," he says after a moment.

"Good night."

A few minutes later: "Lindy?"

"What?"

"Sure you won't join me?"

"I'm sure."

"Arghh." he groans, then starts singing: "I'm so-o-o-o lonesome I could die...." and in a lower register: "I'm so lo-oh-oh-onesome I could die-eye-eye."

"You'll wake everyone and start the coyotes up again if you get any louder," she says.

"But I'm so-o-o-ooo lonely," he moans.

"You'll live."

"I wouldn't be so sure. I've got this condition makin' a bump in the covers. A big bump. Dunno how much bigger it's gonna get. Come up here and take a look."

"Oh, jeez."

"No?"

"No."

She hears a sort of snort that could be stifled laughter; soon his breathing becomes regular, and he's snoring softly.

Lindy, however, lies awake for some time, unable to stop the mental slide show of his solid thighs straining against his jeans; his muscles rippling under the shirt that hugs his broad shoulders and flat stomach; the bounce in his step, the cocky grin that should turn her off but is somehow appealing.

And yes, she has noticed a bump, but in his jeans rather than his blankets. The flutter she got deep inside when he circled her in arms and said, 'gotcha' sweeps over her again.

THE NEXT MORNING, THE other men enquire how Lindy slept. And not just once. She's puzzled to be asked the same question repeatedly, although with variations, but answers patiently.

"Don't pay no attention to these assmeats, Lindy," Red finally intervenes. "If anyone's interested, I'll tell you who didn't sleep good, and that's me. Goddamn, Gorgeous. You got a snore on you like a D8 Cat startin' up. I'm movin' in with Melon or Wiggles tonight."

This starts a discussion over which of them can offer the best accommodation. The bed, the snoring, who can be counted on for the most stimulating bedtime conversation—all topics discussed. Then the discussion turns to whose farts are the stinkiest (not a good thing) or loudest (possibly a good thing) or most musical (mixed opinions about whether that's even possible).

Wiggles is adamant it is indeed possible for farts to be musical and says his are hands down the best, owing to his musical talent. He claims he can even produce treble farts in different notes and has been practicing Ghost Riders in the Sky, in farts. Everyone agrees that's hard to top, but Gorgeous says, "Prove it."

"Not fair to ask me now when you know damn well I just went fer a fart walk," Wiggles says.

"Well, you can't make a claim like that without some proof to back it up."

"Okay then, if we have beans fer supper tonight, I'll demonstrate later."

"It's chili fer supper tonight, so I'll bunk in with Melon, thank you very much," Red says. She shakes her head and looks at Lindy. "Farts. They have to discuss farts at least once a day. Honestly. You'd think they were seven years old."

Breakfast is pancakes, sausages, and coffee. Red, wearing a stained and faded bib apron reading 'Kiss The Cook', declined Lindy's offer of help, and stands by the little stove to serve. When they're finished eating, the men go to take the horses down to water, obediently giving Red a kiss as they pass.

"I'm gonna wear this inside-out from now on," Red complains, but with a smile, as she unties the string at the back of her neck and lets the bib part of the apron fold down.

Lindy is surprised when the men, instead of leading the horses to the creek, clip the lead ropes to the halters and race past the camp without saddles or bridles.

"Look at that." Lindy says. "How do they control them?"

"Well, the horses're used to being ridden that way, plus they want to get a drink so they'd head for the creek on their own if they could. Some might be a little hard to stop with just the halter, but if one should take off, and that'd be Brutus if it was any of 'em, Melon would just ride him until he got tired of runnin.'"

Soon, splashing sounds and hooting and hollering from the creek draw their attention. The horses have drunk their fill and now they're milling about in thigh-deep water in the middle of the creek. The riders are trying to pull or push each other off, jostling for position. It seems to Lindy the winner should be the last one still on his horse, but when Nick is pushed off, as soon as he surfaces he fishes his hat out of the water, swings back up onto Petey and gets right back into the thick of the skirmish.

"How are they going to decide the winner? I thought maybe once you were off your horse, you were disqualified."

"Oh, I doubt they have rules. They'll just keep foolin' around until they git tired of it, or until someone breaks somethin', whichever comes first."

Brutus, the biggest of the four horses, has his ears pinned and delivers bites to the other horses whenever he gets the opportunity. The other horses try to stay out of range, despite what their riders want. It's a definite advantage for Melon, who only has to grab the shirt of a rider whose horse is fleeing ahead of Brutus, turn away, and hang on. Melon unhorses Nick again and Wiggles hits the water seconds later, thanks to being grabbed by the huge fist of the much bigger Gorgeous. Gorgeous and Melon wrestle for a while but break apart when Nick and Wiggles, mounted again, each grab one from behind and pull them both off their horses.

"And this is why they're called cow*boys* "n' not cow*men*," Red shakes her head. "At this rate, the game could go on a while. But after those assmeats are done foolin' around in the creek, I need to go down there 'n' wash a few things. One of 'em bein' my pits. You?"

"Yeah, for sure. It's been so hot, I'd like to wash my shirt, too, but it's the only one I have with me."

"Maybe you wanna wash it, wear yer PJ's til it's dry?"

Lindy shakes her head. "No. My, er, pyjama top is, umm, too skimpy."

"Well, get Nick to loan you one of his shirts, or I've got a T-shirt you can borrow."

"That would be great, thanks. I didn't bring a bathing suit either, but wouldn't mind swimming in bra and panties, if the guys were busy elsewhere. Is the creek deep enough?"

"Might be deep enough in places, and we could swim in our birthday suits because they'd stay away if we asked, but the water's colder than a witch's titty." She points to the still snow-covered mountain peaks in the near distance. "Glacier fed. You can swim if you want to try it, but fer me, I'm happy with a washcloth."

"Maybe if it gets hot later."

"Sure," Red agrees, "although I doubt it'll ever be hot enough I'd want to go in. Let's pick up around here while we're waitin'."

Lindy helps clean up around the site, stuffing garbage in a plastic bag and returning empty beer bottles to their cartons.

"Good," Red says. "Let's sit for a bit. There's coffee left."

They sit on the bumper of Melon's truck and enjoy the warm morning sun on their faces.

"Beautiful mornin'." Red says. "I don't think I'll ever get tired of Alberta sunrises."

The sun's been up for some time. There were rosy pink streaks across the eastern sky set off by clear, deep indigo earlier, but these gradually paled to more pastel tones, still beautiful.

The men, tired of the game now that they're all wet, have come up out of the creek and picketed their horses. Now they're toweling off, shivering and complaining about who did what to whom and how cold the water is. When Melon says he's going to give his tack a good cleaning, the other two men decided it's a good time to do theirs, too, and all three head out.

It's quiet again. The aspen grove and the prairies themselves are filled with birdsong. Despite the occasional shrill whistles from the nearby gopher colony, a calming stillness settles.

"We might be glad for some shade later," Lindy offers. Then she says, "Red?"

"Uh-huh?"

"I was wondering. Do you ever dye your hair?"

Red chuckles. "Is that yer way of askin' why I go by Red?"

"You don't have to tell me if it's too, you know, too personal."

"Naw, it's no secret. But I don't tell everyone." Red has smoked her cigarette down nearly to the filter; she takes one last drag before extinguishing it in the dregs of coffee in her mug.

"I've been lots of places, Lindy. Left school when I was fifteen. I'd been doin' the cookin' at home 'n' had a part-time job bussing tables after school, so I knew a few things, didn't have trouble gittin' a job. Came up to Calgary 'n' worked at a few different places there. Headed to Banff 'n' stayed there a while. Then Merritt. I was on my way to Vancouver, when I got the crazy idea to go to Gibson's Landing instead. I thought to git a job at Molly's Reach, 'n' that I might get discovered. A new star in The Beachcombers. Crazy, huh?"

"Wow. But did you? Were you ever in it?"

"Well, I got the job at Molly's, 'n' the director needed extras from time to time. Guess I mighta been in the background of a few shots. Mostly it was standin' around fer hours on end 'n' gitting paid a sandwich 'n' a Coke 'n' about nuthin' more. They ain't filming all the time, you know. I got laid off Molly's at the end of summer when the tourists left. Had nuthin' else so when I got offered a job as cook on the White Witch, I thought, why the hell not?"

"White Witch?"

"It's a black cod long-liner, seventy-five footer, crew of six. All men. They never would've hired me, or any woman, if they weren't stuck. Anyhow, except for the odd couple nights when we put in to Winter Harbour, we were at sea for months, a hundred miles off the northern tip of Vancouver Island. I made one trip. That was more than enough. I hated it. Rough seas, seasick half the time, pots sloppin' 'n' bangin' around. Never did get used to it. No set pay, just a share of the catch. That trip we nearly got skunked so the crew shares were small. The guys all started callin' me Red like it was a big joke."

"I don't get it."

"Oh, they joked that my crew share was so small, all I got was a red snapper." She chuckles. "That's a fish, Lindy, 'n' you don't git 'em in black cod traps so they were just bein' assmeats. But you know what they meant. Weren't true of course, I had my bunk in the galley 'n' kept my distance. But I kinda liked that name, so I started usin' it."

"Huh. It's cool," Lindy agrees, "better than Princess, that's for sure. My friend's parents call his little sister Princess. She's six. If I have to have a nickname, I wouldn't choose one that makes it sound like I prance around in a ballgown."

"You usually don't pick your own nickname 'n' I think you might be stuck with that one. You think any of the guys picked theirs?"

"I guess not. But you picked yours."

"Only because it's the only name I ever told 'em. And I've been using it so long it's almost more my name than nickname."

Lindy nods and decides against asking what her actual name is. Instead, she asks, "Have you known Nick for a while?"

"Since he joined the tour I guess, six, maybe seven years. He was just a skinny kid then, still in university. I don't see a lot of him. He rodeos here 'n' there. As a rule he don't go far, now with his practice in Edmonton to look after."

"His practice?"

"His dental practice."

"He's a dentist?"

"You didn't know? Why'd'ya think they call him Painless?"

"I must really be dumb, but I don't get that, either."

"Well, one of the old timers came up with it back when he first came on the tour. You know, like how dentists back in the Wild West used to advertise 'Painless Dentistry.'" Red clucks. "Dunno why he's so secretive about it. Everyone knows. He's the closest thing to a doctor that's around sometimes 'n' so of course if someone gits hurt, he's always called on to take a look. Stuck a guy's tooth back in for him once, that's the closest thing to dentistry he's been called on to do, far as I know. So we all know he's a dentist, but it gits his back up if we tell anyone. So don't you let on I told you."

"I won't," Lindy promises. She ponders the news for a couple of minutes, thinking someone his age, so good looking largish nose notwithstanding, and a dentist besides, wouldn't be unattached. She decides to ask. "So, with all the horse girls around, why doesn't he have a girlfriend?"

"Horse girls?"

"Well, cowgirls I guess. I met some in Calgary. Carla and, um..."

Red gives her an odd look, and says, "If you were talking about the barrel racers, I guess you could call them cowgirls, but I know the girls you mean. I doubt they could tell a Quarter Horse from an Arab 'n' I'm pretty sure none of them has ever been on a horse." Red digs a cigarette out of her breast pocket and lights it, dragging deep and exhaling before continuing. "If they was hangin' around baseball players, they'd be baseball Annies; if they hung around outside the stage door waitin' fer rock stars, you'd call 'em groupies."

"Oh." Lindy feels her face getting warm.

"So the girls yer talkin' about, we call buckle bunnies," Red stands, stretches her back, and then turns to look at Lindy. "Sure, he goes with one of 'em once in a while, 'n' they sure go after him hammer 'n' tongs. But when he had a steady girl a couple years back, I don't think he even looked at them. He was so smitten with her, talk about wearin' yer heart on yer sleeve. I don't know what happened there. The split hit him pretty hard, I think. He does his best to hide it, but he's really sensitive, not like some of these other assmeats. Well, these guys we're with are okay, 'n' you got a good guy, Lindy."

"Oh, it's not like that."

"No? What's it like?"

"He's just giving me a ride. Friends."

"Friends, eh? Hmm." She walks off a few steps before turning back and saying, "Don't you go breakin' his heart." She gives Lindy an intense look, then shakes her head and says, "Let me know if you want to borrow a T-shirt." She turns away and heads to the wash-up bucket with her mug.

MELON IS AT THE COFFEE pot when Red brings her mug to wash up. "Makin' a fresh pot," he tells her. "I'm ready fer another cup 'n' likely someone else'll want some too."

"Oh, prob'ly. Here, I'll do it."

"No, it's okay, I got it." He opens the lid on the coffee tin, digs out the scoop, and dumps coffee into the drip basket, then sets the pot on the camp stove and lights the burner. "Looked like you was havin' quite a chinwag with Princess."

"I was. Well, I guess I was doin' most of the talkin', if I think about it. Seems like she's pretty good at gittin' a person to yak."

"You find out what she's up to here?"

"Naw, I told her my life story 'n' she didn't tell me hardly nuthin' about herself. I didn't pry." The kettle on the camp stove still has some hot water in it, so Red adds it to the wash bucket, then washes and dries the half dozen dirty mugs before setting them back on the table. "I think I must be wrong about her bein' Gobbler's daughter. She doesn't seem old enough. Well, I mean, the gal I was thinkin' of hadda have left him twenty years ago, far as I remember. I'm sure it was during the time he was winnin' all the buckles 'n' I think that was twenty years ago. So if she was pregnant when she left, that baby'd be twenty now. Lindy can't be twenty. I mean, she could be, lookin' at her, but if she was, she'd have a job, wouldn't she? Nick said she's a student, but if she's in university, you'd think she'd have something better than babysitting for summer work, but that's it. And she's so naïve. She called the buckle bunnies 'horse girls'. You shoulda seen her face when I set her straight on that." Red chuckles.

"Looks a bit like him don't you think? Could still be his daughter. I'm guessin' there's been a few other gals in 'n' outta Gobbler's camper over the years. Otherwise, still no explanation fer why she's lookin' fer him if she ain't a buckle bunny. I think you should just ask her."

"No, she already said it's personal, so... Well, if I git the chance, I'll ask."

They see Nick come out of his camper and shut the door. A couple of minutes later, Lindy comes out, wearing one of his shirts. She looks at Red with a big grin and holds up a towel. She calls across the campsite, "I'm ready to go down to the creek for a wash any time you are, Red."

"Okay." Red calls back. Then she says to Melon, "One other thing. She says she 'n' Nick ain't a couple. She says he's just givin' her a ride 'n' they're just friends."

"Yeah? So nuthin' goin' on behind that closed door?" Melon nods toward Nick's camper; the coffee's perking nicely so he turns the burner down. "You believe that?"

"I do."

"Well. I guess yer a better judge of that than me. Just friends, eh? Wonder if he knows it."

"If he does, I'd say he's hopin' to change it pretty quick."

THE NEXT DAY, THE COW pie tossing contest ends when there are no intact cow pies left. Gorgeous declares himself the winner. A heated discussion ensues, but when he leaves the group for a few minutes and comes back with a cow pie that's still wet in the middle, promising to throw it at anyone who wants to keep arguing, discussion ends. He hurls it at Melon anyway. Melon looks up at the last second and almost doesn't dodge in time; the pie sails past him and hits the front fender of his truck with a splatter. Melon swears and frowns at the mess, then plunges across the campsite to body slam Gorgeous to the ground. They writhe around for a few minutes with Gorgeous laughing the whole time, until Melon has him in a headlock face down on the ground.

"Say uncle." Melon demands. "Say uncle."

"Uncle! Uncle!" Gorgeous hoots. When Melon gets off him, Gorgeous gets to his feet, and laughing harder than before, points at Melon's hat, which was crushed flat under him.

"That hat's new! It was fifty bucks," Melon shouts. Now everyone's laughing.

"It ain't funny." Melon might have tackled Gorgeous again, but Red pushes in between them.

"Lunch is ready," she says. "You all git yer mits washed 'n' come eat."

After lunch, Lindy declines an invitation to play cards and instead spreads a blanket in the shade of Nick's camper. She pulls a nail file and a bottle of polish out of her purse and spends some time on her nails. Then she gets out her book and reads. Red and Gorgeous are playing cribbage, and Nick, Wiggles and Melon are into a game of rummy.

"I'm tired of sittin' around," Wiggles says after a bit. "I say it's time we put Lindy on a horse."

"Me? No." Lindy says. "I don't know how..."

"Well, you ain't gonna learn any younger 'n' you had yer nose in that book long enough," he declares. He takes the book from her hand and pulls her to her feet. "Come on, now."

Nick fetches Petey from his picket and ties him to the loop on the side of the trailer. He shows Lindy how to tack up. That done, he puts the reins up over Petey's neck and coaches her as she mounts.

"Nicely done, Princess. Yer a natural. Now, Petey's a rope horse, so he can move quick. He won't do nuthin' nasty though. Just grab a hold of the horn till you git the feel of it. If you git scared you kin stop any time just by sayin' whoa. Also if you drop the reins, or lose your balance, he'll stop. Don't pull on the reins, just hold 'em like so," he says. He shows her how to hold both reins in her left hand, the trailing ends in her right, and how to neck rein.

Brutus was chosen from the other three horses for Nick to ride since he needs exercise the most. Melon tacked him up while Nick was getting Lindy organized, and now hands Nick the reins. Nick swings into the saddle and they start away from camp.

"Don't worry, you won't have to steer," Nick tells her. "Brutus might not like it but we'll just walk, 'n' Petey will follow. Petey might have to jog a bit here 'n' there to keep up because Brutus has a bigger stride 'n' walks faster. Just sit quiet 'n' you'll git along fine."

They splash through the creek and on the other side, find a cow path and follow it along the ridge at the top of the ravine.

Living in Calgary, the Gateway to the Rockies, Lindy grew up seeing the blue mountains off in the distance. She'd been to Banff many times, but Banff is in the mountains, rocky and forested, vastly different. And she's never been on a horse. Once she realizes Petey really will walk along after Melon's horse as predicted, her nerves settle and it's exhilarating. The four-beat swaying motion, the horse's head nodding with each step, is peaceful; Lindy lets her hips and back undulate with the motion, and relaxes.

Ahead of her, Nick sits the bigger horse as if he's part of it even though it looks to be a rough ride. Brutus bounces around and tosses his head constantly. Nick says Petey is an old hand and always was quiet but Brutus is young, just five years old, and wants his head, meaning he wants to run. Part of his education is to learn patience. So the sedate pace is a good lesson for him.

The long prairie grass is bleached and dry except for the green strip along the creek; scattered across the landscape are small stands of aspen and silvery shrubs Nick calls buffaloberry, as well as the wild roses Alberta is famous for. With no vehicle exhaust to taint the air, the roses can be smelled from a distance. It's a hot day. The breeze, although warm, is welcome; when it stirs the aspen leaves, they make a pleasant sort of rattling sound.

Lindy breathes deep, then squirms in the saddle, trying to ignore the uncomfortable bulge under her thighs where the cinch's butterfly knots are. She thinks, *tenderfoot? Tender thighs more like it.* At least now her boots are comfortable.

They come to a more open stretch, and Lindy notices clumps of bright orange scattered here and there. She asks, "Are those orange things flowers?"

"You stay put," Nick says. "Just give a little tug on both reins and say whoa if Petey starts to follow." He jogs Brutus off the path and out into the grass; at the nearest orange clump, he dismounts and picks. When he leads Brutus back to stand next to Lindy, he removes his hat with one hand and holds out orange flowers with the other.

"For you, Princess," he grins and executes a sweeping bow.

"Thank you," Lindy says, accepting the bunch. "Beautiful. Lilies?"

"Tiger lilies."

"Wow. They're really beautiful. I hope they don't wilt before we can put them in water." She shifts them awkwardly into her right hand, then back to her left, tries holding the reins with the flowers in that hand while clamping onto the horn with her right.

"Here," Nick says. He takes the bouquet and ties it up in the saddle strings on the back of her saddle before swinging onto Brutus again.

They haven't gone on more than a few yards when a pair of grouse fly up out of the grass very near Brutus. Their wings clack noisily. Brutus spins, scoots sideways for several hops, then starts into a turf-pounding gallop. As predicted, Petey does nothing but give a little twitch and jog a few steps. "Whoa." Lindy says, and he obediently stops.

After galloping way out across the prairie and around a stand of aspens, Nick circles Brutus back and lopes up beside Lindy. "Well," he says, "he should be happy now that he had his run."

"Those birds probably scared me more than Petey." Lindy laughs. "I'm glad he didn't do what Brutus did."

"Brutus wasn't scared, he just used the birds as an excuse to be an asshole. That's why yer on Petey."

"You knew he would do that?"

"No, a'course not, not right then. But he has a spook in 'im, 'n' he's known to bolt. He was lookin' fer an excuse, so—sometime or other, bound to happen."

"That doesn't scare you?"

"Jeez, Lindy, I'm a bull rider. Brutus thinks he's all big 'n' scary but he's got nuthin' on a ton of angry Brahma."

"I guess not. About the bull riding thing. Isn't it kind of crazy to even think about getting on a bull?"

"Don't have to be crazy, but it helps, as they say," Nick says. "Nuthin' quite like it, though. Hard to git an adrenalin rush outta playin' golf after seein' that huge head 'n' them horns bearin' down on ya while yer scramblin' to git off yer ass."

"Well, I wish you'd just stick to the roping stuff. Or maybe the horses, the bucking horses, they don't go after you if you fall off, do they?"

"Aww. Only our third day together 'n' already you care for me."

"Pfft. It's not that, you can go get yourself killed for all I care. Well, I don't mean that. It's just, well, I've been at the Stampede and I've seen the bull riding. At least the horses just run away after you fall off. Bull riding is just not sensible."

"Nope. Not sensible at all. But there ain't nuthin' quite like it."

They ride along in silence for a bit, enjoying the meadowlark songs. An eagle sails on thermals overhead. The rhythmic movement of the horses, the sound of their breathing, farting and occasional blowing; sweeping views of the wide-open skies and rolling hills with snow-capped mountains behind them—it's all peaceful and intoxicating. A sense of well-being settles over Lindy.

"I see why they call it Big Sky Country," she sighs. "This is what it must've been like for the pioneers—or the Indians—I wonder if they rode along this same trail."

Nick ignores Brutus's flattened ears and pushes him close enough to Petey to reach over and pick her hand off the saddle horn. He gives it a squeeze. "Could be. There's trails in here that were used to git to Fort Edmonton. Dunno if this is one of 'em, though."

"Imagine that it is, and we're on the same trails people have used for hundreds, maybe even thousands, of years. They had lives. Loves. They're long gone and the trail remains and it'll be here long after we're gone." Lindy sighs again. "Makes you feel insignificant. We are insignificant, aren't we? In the overall scheme of things."

"Dad used to say we're just tenants of the land. I've never really thought about it, but I guess that's what he meant. We're insignificant." Brutus bobbles away and Nick puts him on the path in front of Petey again.

About an hour out, Nick turns Brutus off the trail and holds up at the edge of the ravine for a moment. He calls back to Lindy, "It's a little steep ahead. Just grab the horn, Princess, lean back, put yer feet out in front of you. Let Petey figure out what to do. It's only a couple of feet down."

He touches Brutus with his heels and the horse jumps without taking another step. Petey shortens his steps, slides a few inches, and hops down. Lindy is jostled but never feels like she's going to fall off. When Nick turns to see how she's doing, she gives him a smile.

They stay on the flat rocks next to the creek until they come to a sandy stretch where there's a gentle trail leading up to the top of the ravine again.

"Looks like we could've come down that trail a lot easier," Lindy points out.

"Where's the fun in that?" Nick says. "You're a trooper, Princess. You did good."

They both dismount and let the horses drink from the creek. Nick loosens the cinch on Brutus's saddle and asks Lindy to do the same for Petey, then he slips the bridles off both horses and leaves them to forage along the creek.

"Won't they run away?"

"Petey won't. Brutus likely won't, but if he does bugger off back to camp, don't worry. We'll ride back double. You can sit in my lap." He manages to make a leer look cute, then heads for a grassy spot under the bank where a few scraggly saskatoon bushes hang over the edge, and stretches out in the shade.

Lindy, happy to be out of the sun for a bit, sits beside him. She pulls her shirttail out of her jeans and flaps it to cool her torso. "There's sweat running down my back. I'm going to have to borrow one of your shirts so I can wash this one again."

"We'll hit a laundromat when we get to High Prairie," Nick says. He picks a blade of grass, sets it between his thumbs, and blows on it to make a loud squawk before discarding it. "I have to say, I'm kinda surprised you didn't pack a few more things. It's almost like you took off without a plan."

"N...no, I had a plan. It's just, I always travel light."

"You mean, you fly all over the world with just what's in yer purse?"

"No, silly. I take a suitcase then. It's just—I didn't want to be dragging a suitcase with me through the Stampede grounds. Why would I? I wasn't planning on, er, I mean I thought I'd link up with, umm, I wasn't planning to leave town, remember?"

"Oh, so you live in Calgary." He sorts through the tuft of nearby grass for a more suitable piece and uses it to make another squawk. "But once you knew you had a ride 'n' didn't have to carry a suitcase, why didn't we go by your place so you could pick up a few things before we left?"

"Umm, I umm ..." Lindy says, taking off her hat and swiping her arm over her forehead. *Walked into that one,* she thinks. "I didn't want to make everyone wait. Hey, I thought these hats were supposed to keep your head cool."

Nick's studying her face, quiet for a moment. Finally, he says, "Well, not them cheap felt things they sell the tourists."

"I'll have you know it wasn't cheap."

"Oh? You got ripped off, then."

She roots him with an elbow.

"Ouch. Anyway, if you ain't noticed, we all have straw hats. Ventilated. See the holes? Makes a difference." He takes his hat off and hands it to her so she can examine it. "Felt's for cooler weather."

"Huh," Lindy says. She realizes the hat was one more stupid thing she shouldn't have bought and is embarrassed. She pushes the feeling away, unwilling to let it spoil the mood.

"Anyway, it's good you have this thing to keep the sun off yer head 'n' face. And," he says with a grin, "there's one thing it's good fer I can't do with my hat." He takes her hat from her and goes down to the creek where he scoops it full of water. He drinks from it, although most of the water runs out over his chin and down his shirt front. He refills it and brings it, dripping, to her. She's reaching for it when he dumps it on her head.

She gives a little squeak. "Goddamn you all to hell, Nick. That's cold."

"Aww, is it cold, Princess? You were complainin' about being too hot, weren't you?" He laughs. After a moment, Lindy chuckles too; he sits back down beside her and starts singing: "Out in the West Texas town of El Paso, I fell in love with a beautiful girl ..."

"I think it's Mexican."

"Hey?"

"I think it's a *Mexican* girl."

"You see any Mexican girls around here?"

"No, but then, this isn't El Paso, either." She's taken his meaning, of course, and feels heat rising to her face. She lays back and locks her hands behind her head. A whiff of b.o. reminds her she's felt sweat prickling her armpits almost from the time they started out. The deodorant that promised to check wetness and odor all day long, hasn't. She brings her arms down and laces her fingers together, resting her hands on her stomach. Maybe the dousing with water has camouflaged the sweat stains. Or maybe Nick won't notice them or the fact she's blushing. "If you're wondering, most songs have more than one note."

"A for effort?" He looks at her over his shoulder.

She smiles back and says, "Well, anyway, it does feel good to be cooled off." She breathes deeply of the fresh, sun-drenched air, listening to the munching of the horses and their occasional contented blowing. The creek gurgles along. The sky stretches blue, without limit, cloudless except for a few wisps of white near the horizon. "What could be better than this?"

"Well, I can think of one thing," he says. He stretches out next to her and turns onto his stomach, leaning up on his elbows. "A kiss from a beautiful girl."

"Oh. A kiss. That's not what I thought you were going to say."

"Aww, Princess, you're breakin' my heart. Like I told you on the day we met, I'm a gentleman."

"You have one? A heart, I mean."

"Ouch." He clutches his heart with his right hand. "I do, but you must not or you wouldn't hurt me like that."

"Oh, go on," Lindy gives him a little push. "Well, Petey seems to like you so you can't be all bad. And you brought me to this pretty place, after all."

He leans over her and says, "It's a pretty place all right." His voice is low as he whispers, "But not as pretty as you."

He bends for a kiss. His lips are soft on hers and she's startled by the jolt of electricity that passes between them. She brings her hands up and wraps her arms around his shoulders. He reaches over her, sliding his hand behind the small of her back and pulls her close.

There's a clatter of horses cantering down the path; Petey and Brutus look up and scoot around a few steps. Wiggles and Gorgeous whistle and hoot as they pull up on the gravel shingle in a cloud of dust.

Lindy pushes Nick away and sits up, feeling her face burn.

"Git yer pants on, you two," Gorgeous hollers. "We're gittin' up a game of five card draw 'n' we need yer money, Painless."

Nick gives an exaggerated groan, then rises and pulls Lindy to her feet. "God dammit, guys. Yer timing's lousy."

"Yer right," Wiggles says. "Sorry Lindy. Shoulda got here sooner 'n' saved you bein' mauled by the big brute, but we rode past yer li'l hidin' place the first time. My Indian scout here is a lousy tracker."

"Shit, you'd've went left on that first wye in the trail, but fer me. Plus, I never said I was a tracker."

"We weren't hiding. I think we should be going back now anyway," Lindy says.

Wiggles and Gorgeous water their horses, then suggest a race back to camp. The winner is to get a kiss from Lindy.

"Well, we ain't gonna gallop," Nick says.

"Well, then, you won't have a chance," Wiggles says. "Gorgeous, looks like it's between me and you. Lindy, can I have a lock of your hair for luck?"

"You didn't ask me if I was agreeable." Lindy says.

"No kiss?"

"No kiss."

"Dammit. Okay, then, Gorgeous, last one back pays the winner's entry fees."

"You're on."

Without warning, Wiggles puts his horse into a gallop. Gorgeous pivots his horse and in a few strides, is right behind him.

"Those idiots," Nick says, watching them race along the path. "It's too far to gallop all the way. Brutus wouldn't bolt that far on his worst day 'n' I'd never run Petey that hard."

"Who do you think will win?"

"Well, not Gorgeous. He outweighs Wiggles by about a hundred pounds. I really doubt they'll run all the way back to camp. I sure hope not, for the horses' sakes."

"What about the kiss? Would they actually ..."

"Don't worry, Princess. It would only happen if you agreed to it, 'n' if you did, it wouldn't be some spit-swappin', mug-suckin' event, just a peck on the cheek, most likely. Unless you were really into it. And goin' by how reluctant you've been to kiss me, as handsome and charming as I am, I'm going to say you wouldn't be into it." He gives her a quick kiss before she can respond, then winks and picks up the bridles.

Petey stands nicely to be bridled. Nick hands his reins to Lindy, then goes to bridle Brutus. The big bay turns his rump and scoots away a few steps, then stops to eat as if Nick doesn't exist. "That was really fuckin' rude, Brutus." Nick calls after him. "Sorry, Princess. I meant, that was really rude. He's goddamn lucky I took that rope off Petey's saddle before we set out so I can't rope him. Now I have to sweet talk the bugger."

Nick follows Brutus through scrub brush and down to the creek, then back again. Brutus lets him come close enough to touch his shoulder a couple of times, but as soon as Nick tries to put a rein around his neck, Brutus scoots away a few steps and ignores Nick again. In a soft, coaxing voice, Nick maintains a steady stream of insults to his looks, brains, and parentage, until Brutus lets Nick walk up beside him to put his bridle on.

"Good thing we're not entered in that race," Nick says when he leads Brutus back to where Lindy and Petey wait. "Now we'll be late for chow besides."

"Is Brutus always so much trouble?"

"Yup. Always."

"Why doesn't Melon get another horse, then? One like Petey?"

"Well, Melon's really into the roping, 'n' Brutus is coming along so he'll likely soon be one of the best rope horses on the tour. Petey can't match him. Fer me, it don't matter. I just dabble in roping anyway. Team roping mostly, if one of the guys can't find someone better." He laughs. "Don't tell me you ain't noticed. I can barely catch a steer when it's just a head stuck on a bale. I once caught an innocent bystander by mistake."

Lindy feels a stirring inside at the memory and doesn't resist when Nick puts his hands on her hips and draws her close, whispering, "But I got still got first prize."

She turns her face up to meet his kiss, his lips soft and warm and growing more demanding.

Brutus gives a sharp tug on the rein and it slips out of Nick's hand; he starts to walk off, rein trailing. Nick scrambles after him and manages to pick up the rein. He turns to Lindy and says, "That was awful nice, Princess. Thank you. Now please excuse me while I go kill this big stupid sonofabitch."

Whatever Lindy might have expected, Nick just gives the horse a scratch on the withers and tightens the cinch. Lindy tightens the cinch on Petey's saddle; Nick checks it, and they both mount. Nick leads the way up the gentle incline to the trail that runs along the top of the ravine and will take them back to camp.

When she comes up beside Nick, Lindy says, "You knew they'd follow us, didn't you? That's why we went down onto the rocks, so they'd lose our trail, isn't it?"

"No flies on you, Princess. I'm just surprised it took them so long. It was a pretty good move, eh?" Nick chuckles. "You feel comfortable? Trust Petey? Think we could jog a bit?"

Lindy is familiar with Petey's jog from when he had to hurry to keep up with the bigger horse on the way out, so she agrees.

Nick nudges Brutus into a jog. Petey follows suit. Still, it's not a fast gait, and the sun is disappearing over the mountains when Nick and Lindy get back to camp.

After untacking and picketing their horses, Lindy pulls an empty milk carton out of a trash bag to make a vase for the lilies and goes to the creek to fill it with water. She sets it on the table next to the Coleman stove as they join the group around the campfire.

"Oh my," Gorgeous observes, "Y'all had time to pick posies?"

The others, of course, have finished eating. Red hands Lindy and Nick each a plate of hash and a slice of bread. "There was pan biscuits 'n' corn on the cob but some greedy bastard ate it all," she says, glaring at Gorgeous.

"This is great," Lindy says. "We're late. If we missed out, it's our fault entirely."

"They was so busy, they lost track of time," Wiggles says. He strums his guitar, picks out a few notes and plays a riff or two. Then he says, "I bin thinkin' 'bout writin' a song. Somethin' 'bout how sweet it is to find a nice li'l place for a nap on a hot day. Out on the bald-ass open prairie. No one else around 'cept maybe a sweet young thaaang." He sighs loudly. "Nice shady spot. Maybe next to a babblin' brook."

"Don't fergit the posies." Gorgeous contributes.

"Since you are all so interested," Lindy says, "Nick was a perfect gentleman. It was a fabulous afternoon. I love Petey."

"Ahh, you love Petey, do you? How are you at playing poker? Maybe you kin win him off Painless." Melon is spreading a plastic tablecloth on the ground, sets a lantern on it, and starts shuffling a deck of cards. "He may be a perfect gennelman but he's the world's worst Stook player."

There's a chorus of agreement.

Gorgeous says, "Yeah, he'll hit eighteen. 'S' true. Don't try'n deny it, Painless."

Lindy turns to Nick and says, "So, Nick, I've been meaning to ask: why do your friends call you Painless?"

He narrows his eyes at her, then says to the group, "I'm so good in bed, when I deflower virgins, it's painless."

Melon calls out, "Didn't know yer dick was *that* small."

"Never had any complaints." Nick counters.

"And you won't long's you stick with virgins." Wiggles says.

"Maybe them gals just think a mosquito's botherin' 'em." Gorgeous says.

SEVEN

Whitecourt, Alberta

Friday, July 23, 1976

En route from their camp on the range to the High Prairie rodeo grounds, they stop for gas and to buy ice to replenish the coolers. There's a cafe sharing the site, so they troop in for lunch.

The cowbell over the door jangles as they enter, but with the clatter of dishes, a crying baby and boisterous conversations in the busy dining area, it's barely noticed. One short-order cook can be seen at the grill behind the pass-through, and one harried-looking waitress circulates through the tables and booths, topping up coffees and taking orders as she goes.

One group gets up to leave, so Lindy and the others slide into their seats, even though the table hasn't been bussed. The waitress looks up and manages to smile, calling out, "I'll be right with you, folks. Just gimme a minute." She heads to the cash register with the group that's leaving. There seems to be a problem settling up, so it's not a simple matter.

Red frowns as she looks around. After a minute, she stands, stacks the dirty dishes on their table, and takes them to the dish pit. She washes her hands, then checks the bills for the meals on the pass-through ledge and asks the man on the other side, "Which is nine?"

He barely looks up as he points to a booth at the front.

Red stacks two of the meals on her left arm, picks up the third with her right hand, and takes them to the table. With a big smile, she asks the customers, "Okay, who gets what?"

With that order run out, she returns to her group, gathers up the remaining dirty dishes and takes them to the dish pit. She comes back with menus under her arm and a dishrag. She wipes the table and sets menus in front of everyone before putting the dishrag away and coming back to sit down.

"Can't you never just sit tight 'n' let someone wait on you fer a change?" Wiggles asks her.

"When it comes to sittin' tight, you're one to talk," Red replies. "Just can't stand sittin' at a table full of dirty dishes. Or seein' someone's meals gittin' cold."

Just then the waitress comes to stand next to her. "Thanks, hon," she addresses Red. "We're a bit short-staffed, as you can see."

"Someone quit?" Red asks.

"Yeah, a few days ago. I had a gal start day before yesterday but she only lasted one day. I guess she was hopin' for better tips. If she'd hung on another couple days, she might've got 'em. We're slammed; a bunch of tourists today goin' to the ice fields, plus folks on their way to High Prairie for the rodeo. I'm guessin' you're in that crowd?"

"Well," Red says, "my friends are. Me, I'm lookin' for a job."

"Well, you just got one." The waitress chuckles, then says, "I'm Bertie," and sticks out her hand.

"Red."

"Glad to meet you, Red. Pay's minimum wage but the tips can be good, you get a meal allowance and there's a couple bedrooms in the back. One of 'em's yours if you want it."

"Sounds good."

"So. Can you start as soon as you have your dinner?"

WHEN LUNCH IS OVER and everyone's getting back in their trucks to head out, Red comes to get her things and to say good-bye. "The bedroom's great," she tells the group. "The only entrance is around the side. No access from the diner, so that's good. Even a little TV room 'n' a washing machine." She turns to Lindy and says, "I ain't gonna say good-bye. I might be tired of it soon's I git myself 'n' my clothes clean, 'n' then I'll pick up with the next bunch of rodeo bums that stops in 'n' wind up where yer goin'. Our paths will definitely cross again. So, it's just until we meet again. And good luck." She hugs everyone, then turns and walks away.

Lindy watches as Red disappears around the side of the building, her little duffle bag in hand. Her head is low and she doesn't turn to wave as she pulls open the screen door and lets it snap closed behind her.

Lindy chews her lip, takes few deep breaths, then turns and heads for Nick's rig.

High Prairie, Alberta

Friday, July 23, 1976

THEY ARRIVE IN HIGH Prairie in the late afternoon, drive through town and head out on the road leading to the rodeo grounds. Nick knows the way without checking the map, and soon they're slowing to turn into the exhibitor's parking lot, pulling up close to where Wiggles and Gorgeous parked their rigs. He parks and checks for his friends, but neither they nor their horses are to be seen. "They're probably puttin' their horses in the barn," he says.

He unloads Petey, sending Lindy with a bucket to find the nearest spigot. She returns while Nick's unhitching the trailer, and finds the horse tied to a loop on the shady side of the trailer. She hangs the bucket where Petey can reach it.

"You gotta grow some muscles, Lindy," Nick says as he comes up beside her. "Half a bucket's barely enough to wet his whistle." Petey proves the point by sticking his head in and draining it.

"He's still thirsty. Maybe I should just take him over to the spigot and let him drink there," Lindy says.

"Naw, it's okay. I'll put him in the barn soon's I get my stall assignment anyhow."

"Why isn't he here?"

"Why isn't *who* here?"

"Don't be an ass."

"Ferget about that old buzzard Princess. You got me."

"*Pfft!* I got you? We barely know each other and anyway, it's not the same thing."

"How's that?"

"Well, I'd never suck face with *him*," Lindy says, and gives a little laugh.

"That don't mean nuthin'. Until last night, which by the way I been dreamin' about ever since, you barely sucked face with me, 'n' I'm way better lookin'."

She sobers, realizing she's stumbled into a corner. If she's not hoping for a boyfriend, why is she looking for him? Can she tell him the reason? What if it gets around and her father gets wind of it? If he doesn't want to meet her, as her mother claims, what would he do? He wouldn't leave town, give up the rodeo, just to avoid her, would he? But what if he did? He left the Calgary Stampede early. Just scratched his rides and left. If he'd leave the world's biggest rodeo, he sure wouldn't hesitate to blow this one off. No, she can't take a chance. She takes a deep breath and mumbles, "It's not like that."

"Well, if yer after him 'cause he owes you money, don't hold yer breath tryin' to collect."

She gives him a long look, turns and takes a few steps away, scuffs at a dandelion in the gravel, then turns back and says, "This rodeo is the best choice, right? Not the most prize money but okay? Easy to get to? Close enough he could bring his own horse, enter the roping without borrowing one? Why isn't he here?"

"Who knows? Maybe he don't like the rough stock contractor. Maybe he figgered he'd git a better ride somewhere else. Maybe he flew to a show in the States. Like I told you, he don't check in with me. I ain't his momma."

"He'd spend money to fly? Just for a damn buckle?"

Nick shrugs. "Sometimes two or three of us throw in together 'n' charter a plane so's we can ride in one rodeo one day 'n' another the next. It just depends on where you are in the standings, how bad you need the points. The schedule. And so on. Maybe him 'n' Porky went together. Porky's rig ain't here neither," he says. "Tell you what. We don't know he ain't gonna show up. It's early yet. He could pull in any second. You keep an eye on Petey 'n' I'll go see if the gals at the show office expect him, since you're so damn anxious to know. I gotta go find my stall assignment anyhow." He turns and takes a few steps away, and then turns back. "You don't really think it's all about the *damn buckle*, do you?" With that, off he goes in the direction of the barn housing the show office, dust billowing out under his boots.

Seems like he walked off in a huff, Lindy thinks, *and now he lets me wait out in the parking lot. Why?* If it wasn't for Petey being here, who knows if he'd even come back. But it didn't seem he was really all that mad. So what's taking so long? She scuffs at a grasshopper with her heel.

Hearing a vehicle, she straightens and strides around Petey to see a late-model brown Silverado crew cab with a large camper and a horse trailer painted to match lurching over the sunbaked ruts. Melon.

She waves, then returns to the shady side of the trailer and sinks to the fender near Petey, who's standing favouring a foot, eyes half closed. He gently nuzzles her cheek, sniffing deeply. She strokes the bristly velvet of his chin. "You really are the sweetest thing," she tells him.

At last, Nick appears at the corner of the barns edging the parking lot, two girls in frilly shirts clinging to his arms. Even at this distance she can see his big grin. The clenching of her insides, the beginning of a burn in her guts, is unexpected. "They're welcome to him." she mutters, and realizes it's really just to convince herself. She stands, turns her back and scratches Petey's withers.

"Hey!" Nick strides up behind her and gives her a pat on the butt, then grins and says, "Lindy, this is Rose," he indicates the shorter, dark-haired girl, "and Jeanette."

Both girls smile and say hi.

"Hello," Lindy responds, mustering a smile."

Nick unties Petey and passes the lead rope to Jeanette. "You all right taking him over to the ballfield to graze for a half hour or so?" When she nods, he continues, "So if you could stick him in his stall in the barn after, that'd be great."

"Sure thing, Nick," Jeanette agrees. "See you later. You going to the beer garden tomorrow?"

"For sure. See you there," Nick agrees with a grin. The girls leave, leading Petey, and Nick turns to Lindy. "Thirsty?"

"No. What did you find out?"

"Shoot, I'm parched. Let's git a beer."

"For Pete's sake," Lindy grumbles under her breath. She goes to the back of the camper, wrenches the door open and climbs in. She pulls the cooler out from under the table, pries the lid off and digs out a can.

"This is all there is that's cold," she says to Nick, who has followed her inside. "What took you so long?"

"I ran into a couple guys I ain't seen fer a while. And the gals in the office were busy," he says, tossing his hat on the table, "They don't know if he's comin' or not."

"Oh. So he's not coming." Her shoulders slump.

"Hey, is that what I just said? Don't worry. He could still show up. You can enter even as late as tomorrow morning."

"Nothing to be done about it I guess." Disappointment washes over her. She sniffs, then shrugs and hands him the beer. "You could've waited outside. I'd've brought this out for you."

"Naww. Think I'll take a nap after this," he replies as he pulls the tab to open the beer. "Help yerself, Princess. Relax fer a bit. We got time to kill."

"Well, we should kill it outside. Otherwise everyone will think we're, you know, doing it."

"Doin' what?"

"You know, *it*." She busies herself putting the lid on the cooler and shoving it back under the table.

"Oh, *it*. Hell, you think they'd believe me if I told them we bin sleepin' in separate beds all week?" He puts his beer on the table and when she straightens, draws her into his arms. As he nuzzles her neck, he presses against her. "Mmmm. You smell good."

"Don't be ridiculous! you know I haven't had a shower or washed my hair or changed my shirt in a week."

"Well, it's just you I smell, then. I like it." He kisses her neck and cups a breast. "Yer so soft."

"And you're so not."

"Told you I been daydreamin' about last night," he murmurs, pushing against her harder.

She backs away as far as possible in the confined space and finds herself pressed up against the bunk with Nick bending to kiss her. She gives him a fleeting kiss then tries to squirm away, but he holds tight.

"Come on, pretty girl, you kin do better than that," he whispers. "Relax." Breath warm and beery, his tongue darts into her ear. They kiss for a bit, then his kisses become more demanding. He opens her jeans and starts working them down.

She stiffens and pulls his hands away.

"What?" he whispers huskily.

"It's too soon." She squirms. "This is too soon. We haven't even known each other a week. Just 'cause we've kissed once or twice doesn't mean... I mean... You know! This is happening too fast."

"Hmmm. Well, we spent more time together this week than we would of in a month of Saturday night dates. And kissed? Kinda more'n kissing last night before you shooed me off to sleep alone, wasn't it? I've been thinkin' about it all day, hopin' we'd pick up where we left off. I'm hot for you, Lindy, beautiful Lindy, you make me so hot." He gathers her into his arms for another kiss. She pushes him, hard, sending him back against the table.

"What's wrong?" he asks, his brow furrowed.

"I told you, you're going too fast." She tucks her shirt back into her jeans and zips up.

"Okay." He moves toward her again, this time grabbing her by the hips and hoisting her up on the bunk. Standing between her knees, he takes her hands. The bunk is high enough he has to look up to make eye contact. "What's wrong? I like you, 'n' lord knows I want you, 'n' after yesterday 'n' the day before, all week actually, but especially last night, I thought you felt the same. I don't see how I could be readin' that wrong."

He's reading me exactly right, she thinks. *I do like him; he's sexy as hell and turns me on big time, like nothing I've experienced before.* She blows a breath out and says quietly, "You aren't."

"What's the problem, then? I mean, you don't fall into the sack at the drop of a hat 'n' I'm glad about that. I respect you fer that. But we're both free, white 'n' twenty-one. What could be better'n a little afternoon delight? We been workin' up to it all week, haven't we?"

Afternoon delight. Sex for the fun of it. Suddenly it seems a gulf of years has opened up between them. *I know he's at least twenty-five, probably even older, but he has no idea how old I am. He thinks I'm closer to his age and that I've been around more than I have.* She evades his intense gaze.

"Lindy," he says softly, when she doesn't say anything for a few moments, "I don't want you to do nuthin' you ain't all in on. But I don't git it. How's today different than yesterday? We done this before."

"No, we haven't. Not this far. I mean—that's far enough. I'm not going to do, er, afternoon delight or morning or evening delight, either."

"No? Well." He stands away slightly, and squares his shoulders and rests his hands on his hips. "I have to admit, I don't git it."

"Well," Lindy begins, drawing a deep breath. "I'm white and I guess I'm free, like you said, but I'm not twenty-one. Not even twenty. I'm seventeen."

Nick steps back and sits on the table. He closes his eyes and gives his head an all-over, vigorous, two-handed scratching, then finger-combs his hair, before looking up at her again. He starts to say something, but Lindy continues, "The other thing is, well, I've never, you know, done, er, *delight*."

After a moment, Nick says, "I suppose you ain't on the pill, then."

She shakes her head, clasps her hands together in her lap and examines them.

Nick gets to his feet and takes the two steps to the door, peering out the window for a bit, saying nothing. After a moment or two, he turns and comes back to her.

"At least you ain't jail bait. I have to admit, I figured you were a little older, 'n' I thought since you were lookin' to hook up with a cowboy, you'd probably been around some." He reaches up and tucks a stray lock of blonde hair behind her ear and kisses her gently. "Let's give it some time. Wait 'til yer ready. But fer now, will you be my girlfriend, like, my steady girl? 'Cause startin' now I wanna tell everyone you are. Okay?"

He helps her hop down off the bunk. "Okay? No pressure, just keep on like we bin doin' 'n' see where it goes?"

"I don't know," she says, "going steady? I have to leave by the end of August and you're going to keep on rodeoing."

"Don't see why we should end it just 'cause you have to go back to school."

"But going steady? We'd be faithful to each other even when we're apart for months on end? You really think you can do that? Hold up your end of it? Jeez, Nick. When you're surrounded by all these gorgeous, umm, *buckle bunnies*?"

They're quiet for a bit, just looking at each other. "I guess it's askin' a lot fer you to trust me, but if you're my girl, you'll be my only girl. And we won't be apart for months at a time. We'll still see each other. Calgary's only a couple hours from Edmonton." He lifts her hand to his lips and kisses her knuckles. "We'll see each other weekends. One more year 'til yer outta high school?"

"We really don't know each other, do we? I'm finished high school. I'm going to university. Queen's, in Kingston. I have to choose my courses pretty soon."

"University? But yer awful young."

"I was accelerated in grade school. Skipped grade three."

"I'm a fool. All week we talked mostly about me, and all I did was gawk at you, puzzlin' how to git you in my bunk, never asked nuthin' 'bout you other than how you take yer coffee." Nick slides onto the seat beside the table and pulls Lindy down next to him, not letting go of her hands. "What is it yer wantin' to be?"

"Don't know for sure. I'll take pre-law I guess, and find out. Which means four years just for my undergraduate degree. Then maybe law school, maybe something else. It's a long time to be faithful to someone you've only known a few weeks."

"Well," he blows out a breath, "Kingston's a fair distance away, but you know there's lots of breaks when you'll be home. I know a little about university, believe it or not."

"Yes, you're a dentist. I know," she admits.

"Which one a' them shitheads told you?" he snorts.

"Well, you do slip out of your cowboy talk fairly often. I could've guessed that you had an education, couldn't I? So, why keep it a secret?"

He shrugs. "I guess I want people, girls especially, to like me for *me*. Warts and all."

"I don't see any warts."

"It's early days."

"I guess." Lindy shrugs. "So. You thought I might like you just for what? Your earning potential? The 'Doctor and Mrs.' on the bank account?"

"You wouldn't be the first."

"Well then, I guess I have something to prove to you, too. And I'm sure I have warts, too."

"Everyone does. I'm bettin' I can live with yours 'n' I guess we'll see if you can live with mine." Then the furrow leaves his brow and a grin tugs at the corners of his mouth. "So, any thoughts on when you'd like to get rid of that pesky virginity?"

The joker is back, Lindy thinks. "Seriously?" she asks.

"Yeah, seriously. You must've thought about it. Are you savin' it fer a weddin' ring?"

"No. Well, maybe. But I don't think so. That's not all of it. I just want it to be *right*."

"How will you know when it's right?"

After a moment, in a quiet voice, she says, "When it feels like there's, I don't know, *more*. A connection. When it *means* something. When I'm in love. When I'm not just a convenience, like a toilet."

"Oooo, that's harsh." Nick, grin gone, looks across the table and out the window, quiet for a bit, before turning back to her. His eyes, now deep olive green and intense, hold hers as he says softly, "But I guess I get it. We just met. We don't really know each other yet, 'n' it might seem like I never take anything seriously. But you can believe me when I say I take *you* seriously. Rodeo's a game. You 'n' me ain't. We've got weeks before you leave, 'n' time after that, too, to see if we make that connection. See if love starts up. All right?"

She nods.

"Good," he says, and brushes her lips with his. "But talkin' about my secret! It's nuthin' compared to yers. Admit it. There's something else besides yer age yer keepin' under yer hat. You really didn't have much of a plan when you left home, did you? No clothes but what's on your back 'n' that fluffy little thing you sleep in?"

"You've seen my baby dolls?"

"Don't worry, I don't come down off my bunk 'n' choke the chicken over you while yer asleep. But them hot nights when I couldn't stay asleep, kept wakin' up thinkin' 'bout how close you were, I'd look down 'n' there you were, covers thrown off, them long legs gleamin' in the moonlight so invitin'! Well, you really ought to give me credit fer my restraint."

She feels the blood rush to her face, looks up under her lashes and then away again.

"Them's called baby dolls, eh? A fine sight, Princess," he says, and chuckles. "But you haven't answered my question. Not bringin' anything with you, or stoppin' by your house to pick up a suitcase—it was more'n just wantin' to travel light, admit it. I'm guessin' if yer just out of high school, you still live at home."

She nods.

"Yer parents don't know where you are, do they?"

Lindy studies the tabletop. He cups her chin and lifts her face but she turns her head and avoids making eye contact.

"I take that as a no. Come on, Lindy," he coaxes softly, "talk to me. You couldn't go home, because if you did, your parents wouldn't let you leave again, ain't that right?"

Lindy takes several deep breaths, blowing out through pursed lips, squares her shoulders and says, "I don't think of Mom and Arthur as my parents, just my Mom and Arthur. I've never met my real father and Mom is determined to keep it that way. So when I found out where he was, right in town, likely down at the Stampede since he's a rodeo cowboy, I left, thinking I'd find him that night. I had to sneak out because she never would've let me go."

She locks eyes with Nick now, watching his expression change as the realization comes to him. "Yup, you guessed it, Cam Larsen is my father. I would've told everyone, but my mother says he doesn't believe he's my father and he won't be saddled with someone else's kid. My grandmother says that's ridiculous, there's no doubt he's my father because I look like him, but my mother says she's imagining things and she only saw him a couple of times so how would she know? I don't know if Mom's right, but I can't take a chance. If your friends were to tell him I'm looking for him! Well, I think my best chance of meeting him is to surprise him."

"I see."

"What do you think? Has he ever said anything about, umm, me?"

"Er—well, I dunno."

"I guess that means he hasn't. So if he never told his buddies about me..." She exhales and bites her lower lip.

"Well, um, he might've told some of the guys. Umm, okay, I guess you need to know, him 'n' me are not actually *buddies* ..."

"But you said ..."

"Yeah, I remember sayin' I was. I saw a beautiful girl lookin' lost. It seemed like a good ice-breaker, you know, put her at ease, get her to talk to me. She was lookin' fer a particular cowboy, but he was already gone, so she might as well have me instead, or so I thought. And it worked 'cause here you are. And now you think I just say what I need to, to get what I want, 'n' you don't know if you can believe me when I say I want you to be my steady." He strokes her cheek. "No, don't deny it, that was yer first thought. I meant it, though. And when I told you that night at the Cantina that Gobbler was my buddy—"

"Gobbler?"

"Long story. I don't know all about it, just that it has something to do with a bad ride years ago. Anyway, Gobbler and me, sure, we know each other, but for some reason from day one he's made it plain he don't like me. He's a sore loser, so when I beat him, I rub it in. Any conversations we have are short 'n' not exactly friendly. He'd never tell me anything personal, probably wouldn't tell my friends, neither. But Porky would know. Maybe Red."

"You can't tell them why I'm looking for him, Nick. It might get back to him and I don't know what he'd do. Would he avoid me? I really don't want to just see him from a distance—blow my chance to meet him. What if he even went so far as to leave town to avoid me? Would he do that? This is the closest I've ever come to meeting him and I can't risk it."

"I can't believe he'd avoid you, but hey, he's Gobbler, who knows what he'd do? Don't worry, I won't tell anyone." He pulls her close for a soft kiss and a reassuring hug. After a moment, he says, "So, yer mom didn't give you permission to leave, but did you at least let her know where you were going?"

"I left a note."

"Well, that's something, but goddamn! I'm aidin' an under-age runaway."

"But I'd never get you in trouble, Nick!"

"I know," he laughs, and chucks her chin. "You gotta learn when I'm just bein' a jerk. But your mom must be worried. There's a pay phone over by the office. You need to call 'n' let her know yer all right." He strokes her cheek and gives her another hug. "Let's do that now, okay? There's tons of quarters in my stook pot, so you can talk as long as you want."

She considers it for a moment, then nods.

He straightens and his silly grin is back. "So, *girlfriend*, just so you know, the age of consent for *delight* is sixteen. So when d'you think you might decide to give it a try, if I may be so bold as to enquire?"

"Not today." She stands and heads to the door, opens it, and jumps down to the ground. As she walks away, she looks back back over her shoulder and says, "You can't stay serious for more than two minutes, can you?"

"Tomorrow?" he calls from the doorway.

"Nope, not tomorrow, either." She turns to face him. "Come on. Show me around."

MELON IS PERCHED ON the picnic table he, Gorgeous and Wiggles "borrowed" from the park across the road and installed in the shade under the tree next to his truck. He sees a truck and trailer raising dust on the gravel road, recognizes it as Porky's and gets to his feet, holding up his hand in a kind of wave.

The rig lurches across the sunbaked ruts and carries on to a cleared space on the other side of the lot. Porky slides out of the cab and slams the door behind him just as Melon walks up.

"You musta got here early, gittin' that choice spot, Melon," he says. "Nice shade. Picnic table."

"Yup. Lucky to git the spot under the trees, but we hadda haul the table over from the park. Prob'ly git in trouble fer that. Oh well, what's the worst they can do? Make us move it back?" He lifts his hat, scratches his head, then resettles his hat before continuing. "Say, you know if Gobbler's comin'?"

"Dunno," Porky says. "We picked up some work at Jackpot this week. Cam is dead set on going to Helena fer the big money. We was done at noon so I took off soon's we got paid. You know Cam, he had to hang around in case there was a game got up with the other hands. If he's on a winnin' streak or if at least he don't lose all his pay, he's goin' to Helena. Otherwise, I expect he'll show up here."

Porky opens the front trailer door and unties his mare, flipping the lead rope over her back. Then he goes to the tailgate, drops it, unclips the butt chain and stands to the side. "Back," he says, and after a moment's hesitation, the sorrel mare backs down the ramp and out of the trailer with a clatter. Porky grabs her lead rope as she does, and leads her to the side of the trailer, where he ties her.

"When will we know?" Melon asks.

"Know what?"

"When he'll be showin' up, if he's going to?"

"I guess we won't know until he either shows up or don't." Porky pulls a tin of Copenhagen out of his shirt pocket. He digs out a wad and packs it neatly between his cheek and gums. "Since when d'you give a shit whether Larsen's coming or not?"

"Well, Christ. Where to start?" Melon again lifts his hat and gives his receding hairline another scratch. "Okay. His daughter's here."

"What?" Porky gives the mare an idle pat before pushing away from her. "What the hell, Melon. *How* the hell?"

"She ain't told no one that's who she is. We picked her up back in Calgary. She was lookin' fer him at the Stampede but he'd already pulled out."

Both men are quiet for a moment.

Porky spews a brown stream into the dust. "You sure she's his daughter?"

"Ay-yuh. Well, I don't know, but Red's sure. Said she remembered a gal who was with Gobbler fer a year or two back in the day. If she had a kid, this one would be about the right age. 'N' we all seen a picture of his daughter."

"Red's here?"

"Nope. She's been with us since we left Calgary, but left off at Whitecourt. You know that Shell station with the little diner?"

Porky nods.

"She got a job there."

"Goddamn, wisht I'd'a stopped there. Wonder if she'll ride with me fer a while," Porky wonders out loud. "Did she ask about me?"

"Yeah," Melon says, "A-course she asked about you, couldn't talk about nuthin' else all week."

"Yeah? What'd she say?"

"Oh, the usual. When's that asshole gonna grow up? Why don't he grow a moustache so he could be handsome like you, Melon? That kinda stuff. Shit, Nancy! Whadda you think?"

Porky snorts, "I think yer an asshole," scuffs his boot in the dust and spits another brown stream.

"Anyhow, we all seen that picture Gobbler shows around, but couldn't remember her name, so we ain't a hunnert percent sure. You know what her name is?"

"Hmm. Linda or Lindy, something like that I guess."

"Well, it's her then, although her last name ain't Larsen or we woulda clued in. She's good lookin'. Tall. Favours him I guess. Seems nice, though, which ain't like him, so you can see why we ain't sure she's related," Melon says. "Wasn't raised by him if she is his, that's fer sure."

"He ain't all that bad."

"Yeah, he's that bad." Melon shoves his hands into his front jean pockets, then pulls them out and scratches his head again.

Porky frowns at him. "Goddamn it, Melon, you got lice? Spit out whatever it is yer still chewin' on."

"Well. Umm," Melon clears his throat. "She's with Painless."

"Ho-lee shit." Porky spits his entire wad into the dust, barely missing Melon's boot. "He finds his daughter after all this time and she's with *him*? He ain't gonna like that." He tugs the horse's lead rope to undo the knot.

"You think I don't know that? Wait'll you see what they're like. I seen 'em over at the pay phone. She was hunched over the phone, talkin' all hushed like. He was just shufflin' around, waitin', tryin' not to make it obvious he was eavesdroppin' I guess. When she gits off the phone, she looks like she's bin cryin'. He smooches her fer a while then takes her hand, hauls her over to where I'm sittin' with a couple other guys, 'n' says somethin' stupid like 'I want you to meet my girlfriend' like I ain't just spent a week campin' out with the two of them 'n' then they both laugh 'n' now fer some reason they can't keep their damn hands off each other. Worse'n ever."

"Nope, he ain't gonna like that ay-tall. I don't wanna be the one to tell him."

"Well it sure as hell ain't gonna be me. And you sure as hell don't wanna have them come face to face, all surprised like. What d'ya think happens if they walk up to Gobbler 'n' Painless says 'I want you to meet my girlfriend,'" Melon says in falsetto. "How'd'ja think that would go? You know Gobbler'll start somethin', Gorgeous'll be in it in a heartbeat 'n' we'll have to break it up 'n' prob'ly end up in a bloody brawl. I don't hafta tell you, ol' Gobbler would git the shit beat outa him."

"What did I do to deserve this?" Porky looks at the sky. Then he shakes his head and stomps away. The mare jogs a few steps to keep up.

"I dunno what any of us done," Melon calls after him. Then he says to no one: "Wimmen. Nuthin' but trouble. I shoulda stayed in Calgary 'n' made brownie points with my wife."

EIGHT

Calgary, Alberta

Friday, July 23, 1976

Marie is in bed, still in her nightgown, when Arthur gets home from work. There's a heap of used Kleenex overflowing the night table and spilling to the floor; the room is stuffy, and the heavy drapes are closed.

"Are you sick, Marie?" he asks, coming into the gloom; he strides to the window, finds the pull cords and reefs the drapes open. A flood of hot summer sunlight pours into the room. Marie covers her head.

Arthur comes to stand beside the bed, pulls the covers back to feel her forehead and notes her puffy, red eyes. "You don't feel warm."

"Well, I *am* sick." she snaps. "Sick with worry."

"Still nothing from Lindy, then?"

She turns away from him and shakes her head. "It's been a week."

"Well, not really, not until Sunday," Arthur corrects her. "You know what her note said."

"What if she can't get home? She's got no money. What if she didn't find him. What if she *did* find him and he's not letting her go?" she sobs. "Or worse—leaving in the middle of the night like that, anything could have happened. She could be dead."

"Come on, Marie. That's ridiculous. Stop borrowing trouble." Springs groan quietly as he sinks to the bed next to her. "You're letting your imagination run away with you. It wasn't the middle of the night. She might have gone with friends."

"You know that's not true. Even Glen doesn't know where she is. He didn't take her anywhere."

"If she was dead, there'd be a body and it would be on the news."

"Not if the body hasn't been found yet or she's been taken away somewhere," Marie sobs.

Arthur rubs her shoulder, but she shrugs him off. "Come on," he says, "get up. Have a shower. Get dressed. You'll feel better. We'll go out for dinner. How about The Keg?"

"I think I should call the police."

"Marie, we talked about this. You call the police. Show them the note that says she'll be back in *a week or so*. You know they won't do anything and even if they did, they wouldn't be able to find her. She won't really be missing unless she doesn't come home next week."

"Next week?" She sobs harder and buries her face in the pillow.

Arthur looks at his wife's heaving body and shakes his head.

"Dad!" Jillian yells from downstairs. Then louder: "Dad!"

Arthur gets up, goes out to the top of the stairs and looks down at his Jillian. "What?"

"I'm hungry, and again tonight, there's no dinner," she replies.

"No? How about making yourself a sandwich?"

"I don't see anything to make a sandwich out of, and anyway, I don't *want* a sandwich again tonight." She sticks out her lower lip.

"Well," Arthur says, "I think we're going out for a bite. In about half an hour."

Frowning, Jillian crosses her arms and stamps her foot in frustration. "She's going with us when she hasn't been out of that room all week?"

"Half an hour."

She stamps her foot again, harder this time. "Fine. Half an hour." She turns and goes down the three steps to the foyer, and stomps away.

Arthur goes back to Marie and coaxes, "Come on, Marie. Get up and get dressed. Enough moping already. We're going out for dinner."

She mumbles into the pillow.

"What's that? I didn't understand you."

She turns her tear-streaked face toward him. "That's right, you *don't* understand me. You don't *want* to understand me. I said, I'm not going. I have to be here in case Lindy comes home. Or phones."

"It's not even a week, for Pete's sake Marie. She's a big girl. She can take care of herself."

"You wouldn't be so blasé if it was Jillian. But of course Jillian never does anything wrong, and Lindy never does anything right. Tell me again how Jillian would never do anything like this, why don't you? That really helps. Remind me how Lindy wouldn't've done this if I'd listened to my mother and let that asshole who's her father into our lives. That makes me feel better too."

"I don't know what's gotten into you, Marie," Arthur scowls.

"And you're right. Jillian wouldn't go looking for her mother, would she?"

"Don't be ridiculous, Marie. You know she's dead."

"No, she isn't. She may have passed away, but she's certainly not dead. She's everywhere in this house. Still haunting this hideous house. Besides, Jillian is *never* going to leave home."

"This hideous house? Haunting? And why would Jillian leave when we've got all this room? Marie, you're not making sense. You need to calm down."

"I'm not going to calm down. Go. Take your obnoxious toddler with you." She turns back to the pillow.

"Now, that's uncalled for."

"Shut the door behind you."

For a heartbeat, Arthur stands, hands on hips, nostrils flaring, just looking at her. Then he draws a deep breath, shakes his head and leaves the room, closing the door as instructed.

In a few minutes, Marie hears the garage door opener and the Cadillac hums to life. When she hears the garage door close and the car drive away, she gets up to use the toilet. She thinks maybe a shower is a good idea after all; pulls her nightgown off over her head, then stands under the water, shampooing and soaping until the water starts to run cold.

When she gets out, she dries herself off, then wraps the towel around her head, struggles into a dressing gown and goes back to the bed. The bed's a mess, sheets rumpled, pillow flattened. She pulls at the bottom sheet to smooth it, pulls the towel off her head and lays it across the pillow, then lies on her back and dozes off.

The phone on her bedside table jangles, waking her; she rolls to her side and grabs it on the second ring, pulling it onto the bed. "Hello?"

"Hi, Mom."

NINE

High Prairie, Alberta

Saturday July 24, 1976

I t's 7:30 A.M. From the narrow window in the bunk of his camper, Cam Larsen sees riders, rodeo organizers and lookey loos milling around the door to the rodeo office. It's nearly time for the draw.

He's running behind. He got in late and has only had a couple hours' sleep. He wishes he hadn't stayed in that poker game as long as he did, a wish he's had more often these past few years. At least, and as usual, he slept in his clothes so that saves time. He slides out of his bunk, careful not to make any movements that might jostle his head, and thinks, *great, I've got the mother of all hangovers. Again. Need a little hair of the dog.*

There's the neck of a bottle showing between the cushions; he pulls it out, clucking when he sees there's only a few mouthfuls left; then he shrugs and rinses his mouth with it as he gives his teeth a perfunctory scrub with the toothbrush lying next to the stove. *Good thing about using rye to brush your teeth,* he thinks, *is you don't need nowhere to spit.* He finds his boots and pulls them on over holey socks.

Now he urgently has to pee. "Next rig," he mutters, "gonna have a head." He could use the sink, but it's full of garbage, dirty dishes and maybe that cloth sticking out is last week's gaunch waiting to be washed out. Still... But the idea is too repugnant, at least when he's sober.

He picks his hat off the stove, settles it on his head, and shoves the camper door open, then climbs out onto the tongue of the trailer. He squints his eyes nearly shut against the bright sunlight, and hops to the ground. A needle of white hot pain shoots through his knee and it nearly gives way, causing him to groan and put a hand back on the camper to steady himself. *That's gittin' worse,* he thinks. *Useta only flare up in rainy weather. Hot all week 'n' ain't got better.*

He unzips, pulls out his penis and sends a stream of urine into the dust near the closest tire. There's a grasshopper scrunching down getting ready to launch; he aims for it but misses and splashes urine-mud on his boot. "Perfect. Goddamn perfect," he mutters.

He straightens and half-turns as he zips up, only then realizing there are two women standing not ten feet away at the camper next to his, watching him. Each has a mug and a cigarette and both are frowning. One makes a comment under her breath; they both cluck and shake their heads. He considers asking them if they'd like a closer look at his cock, want to take a picture maybe, but one he doesn't recognize is good looking and he might want to see more of her, and the other is the wife of one of the ropers. He doesn't care about that too much as a rule, but if she's married she likely won't want to fool around, or if she does, it'll be a shit load of trouble. Whatever. With his pounding headache, he doesn't want the noise of that many words in his head. Instead, he tips his hat and mutters, "Mornin'." He gives them what he hopes is a winning smile and congratulates himself on being civil, given his present condition and the fact they both look like they're sucking on lemons. Or maybe have their mouths full of shit. At that thought, he chuckles despite himself and walks around the front of his truck.

He can't remember what he did with his horse the night before. He's not in the trailer or he'd have been banging around in there before now. He thinks he put him in the barn near other horses. Porky would recognize Diamond, give him some water, maybe toss him a flake of hay. *Can always count on Porky to do the right thing,* he thinks.

He spots Porky in the main parking lot beside Melon's rig. There's a picnic table there, too, and other cowboys standing around. Melon? Gorgeous? Wiggles? Why aren't they over at the rodeo office with everyone else? More to the point, why is Porky hanging around with those assholes?

Normally he wouldn't even acknowledge them, but he has to walk past them to get to the barn to see if Diamond's in there. Porky probably knows where Diamond is, might as well say something to him, so he points his feet in their direction.

As he approaches, Porky comes toward him and sticks a Styrofoam cup of lukewarm coffee in his hand.

"Mornin," Porky says. "'Bout time you woke up."

"What the hell?" Cam responds.

"Mizzable as ever, I see."

Cam asks, "What goin' on? Someone die?"

"No, nuthin' like that."

"'Least not yet," Gorgeous mutters.

"What's that, Gorgeous?" Cam demands, taking a step toward the big cowboy.

"Oh, he don't mean nuthin," Porky says. He puts a hand on his friend's chest and guides him toward the table.

"Goddamn it Porky. Somebody. Shoot."

Porky sends a wad of tobacco spit into the dust. He lifts his hat and gives his face a wipe on his sleeve, then resettles his hat. "Gonna be a hot one..."

"Yeah, yeah," Cam snarls, "we're all hangin' 'round here jawin' while everyone else is gittin' ready fer the draw 'cause it's gonna be another hot day? Goddamn it Porky."

"Is them the only three words in yer vocabulary? Oh I know. A goddamn five-dollar word. Just 'cause it's got more'n two syllables. Okay. Yer daughter's name is Lindy, right?"

"Yeah. What the hell?" He feels a rush of concern. "Has something happened to her? Is she okay?"

"She's not only okay, she's here 'n' she's lookin' fer you."

The others are all nodding, giving Cam a fleeting mind-picture of the Hula Girl bobblehead doll on his dashboard. Then the news washes over him. "Oh gawd," he exclaims, and abruptly sits on the table, sloshing coffee onto his jeans. He barely notices it. Instead he puts the cup on the table and stands again. "Where is she?"

"Errr," Porky begins, "there's more."

Cam scans their faces, opens his hands, and with a slight shake of his head, asks, "What?"

"Well," Porky takes a few steps away, then says, "she's with Painless."

With surprising speed, Cam closes the distance to Porky, grabs his shirt front, and demands, *Where is she?*"

"Goddamn it, Gobbler. Yer shithouse breath's enough to gag a maggot. You look like a hunnert miles of bad road. You gotta git yerself cleaned up before you meet her."

Cam grips his shirt tighter. "How'd she git hooked up with you? What's it got to do with these assholes? You let them—"

"He didn't know anything about it, Cam. In fact, we didn't know who she was when we picked her up," Melon says.

Cam drops his hands but doesn't step away from his friend.

Melon continues, "Red figgered it out. But Painless still don't know. We couldn't figger a good time to tell him. Maybe now's as good a time as any. So, I say we send Lindy into town to git groceries. Then we all go to the draw. Then you go git showered and shaved at least. You and me must be close to the same size. I got a clean shirt you can borrow if you need it."

"And maybe brush yer teeth a couple times." Porky says.

"Goddamn it, Porky."

"We ain't got much time. Melon, kin you go explain to Painless? I'll keep this asshole outta sight till the coast's clear."

Melon nods and hurries off.

Gorgeous clears his throat and says, "We took care of yer horse."

Cam nods at him, picks up his coffee and mutters something about it being cold. "Wouldn't of been if you showed up at a reasonable time," Porky says. "Let's go check on the horses."

Cam glowers, drinks the coffee at one go, belches, then crumples the cup and tosses it on the table before falling in beside his friend, heading for the barn.

"By the way, buddy," Porky asks quietly, "You got moolah for entry fees?"

"I'D LIKE TO GO WITH you to look at the bull you're riding this afternoon," Lindy tells Nick as she's clearing the picnic table of empty coffee cups and concession-stand breakfast burger wrappers. If Red was here, she'd have made breakfast. Lindy offered, but the guys said they needed groceries first; they got breakfast from the concession and then sent her away to shop. When she put the groceries away, she found a couple packages of sausages and plenty of pancake mix, so their real concern must have been her assumed lack of cooking skills.

She smiles to herself as she stuffs the garbage in a bag and realizes she's slid into Red's role as camp slave. It's as if the guys expect it, and that would normally get her back up, but she finds it's comfortable even though it's sexist. They've insisted on paying for everything, after all, even her lunch at the diner yesterday and breakfast sandwich from the concession this morning. Then they each chipped in a ten-dollar bill and sent her off in Nick's truck to get groceries at the Safeway store near the fairgrounds while they went to the draw. Taking over Red's duties, doing her part, is surprisingly enjoyable. She's accepted into the group. It's a comfortable feeling.

"Yup," Nick says, "I think we all wanna go see."

There's agreement all around and the five of them head over to the stockyards. After they've gone fifty yards or so and Nick says nothing more, Melon, walking next to him, roots him with an elbow.

"Uhh," he stammers, "Lindy? There's somethin' we have to tell you."

They stop walking and cluster around her.

She cocks her head, curious. "What?"

"Well ... umm ... Cam Larsen's here. And it's all arranged, we're all gonna have lunch together at the picnic table."

Lindy's jaw drops, then she shrieks, "Great. Great. *Great great great*." She bounces around in a circle, then throws her arms around Nick and kisses him several times. "Thank you, thank you, thank you! I'll put together some real nice sandwiches, with Dee John mustard. Awesome! Awesome! Awesome!"

Then she sobers. "Does he know I'm here? I mean, is he expecting just you guys or does he know..."

"Trust me, if he thought it was just us guys, he'd've laughed his head off," Nick says, and gives her a hug. "Even if he was flat broke, he'd probably starve before comin' to have lunch with us. Lindy, he knows you're here. And we know he's yer father."

She gives him a pointed look and is about to say something, but he stops her by saying, "I didn't tell them. They figured it out the first day, or at least Red did. Of course they didn't bother to tell me." He takes a moment to glare at the others. "I don't blame them; they were worried about, you know, him and me not always seein' eye to eye."

"That's puttin' it mildly," Gorgeous says.

"But why didn't you tell us?" Wiggles asks.

"Well, he... my mom said... It's complicated. Please don't take it personally." She heaves a sigh. "But are you guys sure he's okay with meeting me?"

"He shore is," Melon says. "So don't worry none on that account. He even knows about yer boyfriend here, 'n' he's promised not to be a dink about that. Pardon my French."

She's smiling again, then she sobers and tells them, "It's just, you know, I've never met him."

Gorgeous and Melon shuffle their feet and clear their throats.

Wiggles says, "Aww." He reaches out and gives Lindy's shoulder a rub.

"It'll be okay, honey," Nick tells her, and kisses her temple. "Let's go look at the stock. We need to watch our bulls fer a bit, see how they act, git an idea of their personalities. Then we can take in a few of the early events. We got a couple hours to kill before lunch time."

IT'S 1:00. LINDY MADE a tray of sandwiches, some bologna with Dijon, some tuna, and even egg salad, the latter two with lettuce. She resisted the impulse to cut them in triangular thirds, reminding herself they're for hungry men who might even rather not have them cut in half. They're in Melon's camper, away from the sun and flies, awaiting Cam Larsen's arrival. Gorgeous, Wiggles, Melon and Nick, at the picnic table, are on their second cups of coffee and getting antsy, muttering among themselves.

At last, Lindy sighs, gets to her feet and says, "Well, I think we've waited long enough." She climbs into the camper and comes back with the tray, placing it on the table. "Anyone want something else to drink? There's Coke and ginger ale."

"What? No beer?" Gorgeous asks.

"Beer? When you're getting on a bull in a couple hours?"

"Shit, Princess, you don't think anyone would get on one if they was sober, do you?"

Everyone chuckles at Lindy's frown. She shrugs and says, "Well okay, it's your funeral. But you know I didn't get more beer this morning, so you're going to have to make do with what's left, whether it's your personal favourite brand or not."

Then Gorgeous nods toward the barns, and they all turn to see two cowboys coming their way. Everyone stands as the newcomers approach and stop about ten feet away.

"Ahem," Melon clears his throat. "Lindy, these here's our friends, Mr. Stu Pedersen and Mr. Cam Larsen. Gents, this here's Miss Lindy Jones."

Cam removes his hat and stares at his daughter.

She stares back. *Oh my god,* she thinks, *he is so handsome.* Tall and lean she knew from her one glimpse of him as he was trotting from the house to his truck. But broad shouldered and so well-muscled he looks to be in his thirties instead of his forties. In his spotless white shirt, with his deep blue eyes and even white teeth, blonde hair and skin lightly freckled and tanned, he reminds her of Paul Newman in Butch Cassidy and the Sundance Kid.

"How do you do?" He takes a few steps closer and sticks out his hand.

She steps up and takes his hand to shake; but instead of releasing it, he holds it in both of his, brings it to his lips and kisses the knuckles. She looks deep into eyes so like her own and after a heartbeat, he says, "Lindy. My baby girl. I swear I didn't know 'bout you until 'bout two years ago. I'm sorry. So sorry."

"Mom never told you?"

"Honest to god, no. Was yer gramma told me, a couple years ago. I bin tryin' to git to meet you ever since."

"You came to our house."

"Bin there twice. Called, too. Ever since I found out." He releases her hand, gets his wallet from his back pocket and digs out what she recognizes as her grade eleven yearbook photo.

"Lindy, I would've liked to be in yer life. Seen you at Christmas. Yer first day of school. First date. You musta been cute as a button when you were little 'n' I missed it. Yer a beautiful young woman already 'n' I don't even know you."

She hears Wiggles on her right, honking into a handkerchief, and it brings a little smile to her lips. *Wiggles,* she thinks, *you are such a sweet man. And Mom, you've got so much to answer for.* "I..." she sighs and takes a deep breath. "Well, the best we can do is to start getting to know each other now. We have years, a lifetime. Come. Have a seat. We were just waiting for you before we started eating. You know my friends? My special friend Nick Wilson?"

She turns to the group and is surprised to see that Nick, normally front and center with some smart comment to make, is hanging back. No silly grin. She waves him over. "Nick, come and meet my Dad."

He walks forward but stays several feet away. "We know each other," he says.

"Yes, I know you do. But, well, you've been introducing me all over the place. I want to introduce you. My first time introducing anyone to my Dad. Dad, this is my friend, my *boyfriend*, Nick Wilson." She takes Nick's hand and pulls him to her.

"I heard," Larsen says, frowning. "Just tell me one thing, Lindy. You love him?"

"Not yet," Lindy laughs, "but movin' in the right direction."

TEN

Bull Riding – First Go-Round

High Prairie, Alberta

Saturday July 24,1976

Being with the competitors, Lindy is privileged, allowed to stand on the platform behind the chutes to watch the rides. Remembering all the talk around their little group at the picnic table last night, she's bursting with inside knowledge of what things are called, what's a good ride, and how the judges score the bull and the cowboy each up to twenty-five points, which is then doubled to get a percentage score.

Across the infield the stands are full of paying spectators. She paid nothing and has the best seat, or more accurately, the best place to stand in the house, just a few yards from the bulls, looking down on them. She has a fine view of the goings-on as the riders climb onto the rails and lower themselves onto their backs.

The first ride goes without a hitch; the cowboy stays on to the horn and lands on hands and knees when he goes off. The bull makes only a token lunge at him before being chased into the catch pen. Lindy applauds enthusiastically along with everyone else.

Then a big brown bull comes roaring in, charging the pipes of the chute in front of him, bellowing in rage, trying to climb out before the rider even gets on the rails above him. When he calms, the cowboy begins to settle on him, but he bellows and thrashes around some more. Besides the flankers, there's Gorgeous on one side and another cowboy on the other; they have the rider by the arms, making sure if he gets knocked off the rails he doesn't fall under the writhing, lunging bull. Once the bull quiets enough, the cowboy lowers himself onto his back again. He gets his hand into the rope and pounds his fingers down firmly. Lindy is close enough to see him take a couple of deep breaths before he nods.

The gate is pulled open and the bull lunges out. His shoulders have barely passed the opening when he rears and goes nearly straight sideways as if he's deliberately trying to smash the rider into the chute. The rider is off balance; a twisting kick out behind and he's sent crashing into the fence, landing in a heap on the ground not a yard from where he started.

The bull, now riderless, but still wearing the bull rope and flank strap and still full of rage, charges the nearest horse then trots a few steps off, turns and sets his sights on the cowboy on the ground, and paws. One of the clowns runs in front of him, waving a large red bandana, creating a distraction so Nick and a couple of the other cowboys can safely go to help; the cowboys working the arena keep the bull busy, trying to drive him away. When he finally runs into the catch pen, the clown makes a big production of striding back and forth in front of the stands, mopping his face with the bandana before shoving it back in the huge floral-print pocket on his hip.

Meanwhile, the cowboys huddle over the unmoving rider; after what seems like an eternity, he stirs and sits up. In a minute or two, he is helped to his feet, Nick on one side and Gorgeous on the other, with his arms over their shoulders and their arms around his waist. Sighs of relief course through the crowd. They applaud enthusiastically.

"Looks like he's okay, folks," the announcer says. "By the way, some folks reported seeing Dolly Parton in the stands a few minutes ago. We checked it out, but it turned out to be two bald men sitting together."

Everyone laughs but Lindy's early enthusiasm has dissipated, and she feels sick to her stomach wondering how she can take a whole afternoon of this.

Nick glances up at her as he and Gorgeous practically drag the fallen cowboy behind the chutes where the paramedics await. His expression is grim. Barely out of sight of the spectators, the rider collapses. They carefully lay him on the ground and the paramedics take over.

Nick and Gorgeous rejoin the group of cowboys awaiting their rides. No longer exhilarated, Lindy is filled with dread. Watching bull riding from halfway up the grandstand at the Stampede never brought home the danger like seeing it from where she's standing does. People she knows and cares about are going to take their turns at this? They could be killed before they're even out of the chute.

She studies Nick down below with the other riders. He's with the small group, brushing and checking his rope. Her father is in that group. She hears him say something about rosin, and one of the others hands him a bar. Wiggles is off by himself, sitting on his heels; eyes closed, he appears to be either singing or praying.

Lindy realizes each has his own way of getting psyched up for his ride. Knowing how important it is for him to be able to concentrate on what his bull is doing for eight interminable seconds, she hopes Nick, who's up next, isn't put off his game by what just happened to this other cowboy.

An official says something to Nick as a white bull with a sprinkling of black spots on his back is prodded into the chute. Nick nods, then he, Gorgeous and Melon climb the rails and Nick lets himself down onto the animal. Gorgeous is pulling his rope up tight; Nick rubs it up and down several times, then organizes it, using his left fist to pound his gloved fingers down. Once he settles his hat, he nods.

The gate swings open and the bull charges out, leaping and kicking. It heads out in a nearly straight line in a series of rears and kicks and only jumps off a little to the right a couple of times. Lindy overhears the cowboy standing near her say something about it being a north-south bull; that it's an easy ride and he won't get the big score. It doesn't look easy to Lindy.

At the horn, Nick gets bounced off, landing like he just belly-flopped, but in an instant he's on his feet, easily dashing to the fence ahead of a half-hearted charge from the bull, who seems more interested in finding the catch pen. Lindy lets out a breath she didn't know she was holding. His score is 81.5. It's less than the first cowboy's score, but Lindy thinks it doesn't sound bad; she would have been okay with that if she got it on a physics exam. But from the look on Nick's face, he's not happy. Then he smiles and gives the crowd a wave.

Lindy scuffs a clump of dried mud off the floorboards, and notices the ambulance leaving the rodeo grounds. She takes several deep breaths trying to dispel her worry. Nick's ride is over, of course, and Melon doesn't ride bulls, but that still leaves Wiggles, Gorgeous, and her father. Three more rides to somehow get through.

A couple of cowboys she doesn't know come next. Neither makes it to the horn. It's not as bad as watching Nick's ride, but it's still gut-wrenching to see them dumped and chased by those devils. She can't understand why anyone would want to do this.

Then Gorgeous is on the rails, lowering himself down onto a black bull. It leaps out of the gate and although his kicks are really high, making his back almost perpendicular, it's almost more of a rolling run. Lindy thinks, *oh good, another north-south bull, an easy ride.* Then the bull plants his front feet and deaks to the left, and Gorgeous is half off, barely holding himself on the bull's side. One more big kick and Gorgeous is dumped in the dirt on his shoulder with his feet in the air. The bull kicks out and jumps over him, missing his head by what looks to be mere inches. The horn goes a fraction of a second after he hits the ground. No score for Gorgeous today. Missed it by two-tenths of a second.

Wiggles has a better ride; his bull leaps, spins, then goes bucking but mostly straight with just a few changes of direction. Wiggles clings to him. When the horn goes he's tossed off, but lands on all fours. He scrambles to his feet and has a little bit of a run around with the clowns and the bull before he makes it to the fence. One of the clowns escapes to safety by leaping into his barrel, which the bull then rams a couple of times before he's chased to the catch pen.

Wiggles gets a score of 82. Now Lindy understands why Nick wasn't happy with his score. He's likely thinking ahead to all those evenings in the bar or around the campfire when Wiggles will no doubt talk about the day he beat Painless, in the nicest, most oblique way of course. Knowing Wiggles, he'll write a song about it.

Cam Larsen is next. He makes a show of chatting and laughing with everyone, even calling out to those on the viewing platform where Lindy stands. He blows her a kiss. His bull, a huge beige one with a massive hump and horns pointing down alongside his head, comes charging into the chute. The cowboys around her saw Larsen acknowledge Lindy and they glance at her, muttering quietly. She overhears enough to understand that they know this bull. He's a tough one. A spinner. Lindy sees a flicker of what looks like fear before her father fixes a neutral expression onto his face and climbs out onto the rails above the bull.

Porky and another cowboy are on the rails with him, ready to grab him if the bull thrashes around too much while he's getting ready. The bull seems quiet. Cam settles, gets his glove and rope organized, then nods and the gate flies open.

The bull, so quiet a heartbeat earlier, explodes. He leaps out of the chute and kicks out, his back feet a yard and a half off the ground, then starts spinning. He twists and spins and leaps. At one point, there's a good foot of daylight between Cam's backside and the bull; he loses his hat, pulls himself back in and stays with him through more dizzying spins and leaps. The bull plants his front feet and twists the other way. Still Cam hangs on. At last the horn sounds; he flicks the knot on his rope and half jumps, is half bucked off, landing on hands and knees before rolling away. The bull snorts and chases everyone nearby including the pick-up rider but soon gallops to the catch pen.

Cam gets to his feet and salutes the applauding spectators with both arms in the air as one of the arena cowboys brings him his rope and hat. His score is 85.0, putting him at the top of the leader board ahead of Wiggles and the cowboy who rode first, with Nick in fourth place.

And that's how the go-round ends, because the final cowboy is off after just three seconds.

The announcer says, "That's it for this go round. Four bulls rode, and six cowboys bucked off. To find out who will be cashing the big cheques for the combined scores, come back for the second go-round tomorrow. And now we'll have a short intermission while they harrow the arena and the crew sets up for ladies barrel racing, should be starting in half an hour so you got time to go get a cold drink or treat yourself to some of the other goodies at the concessions, run by the local Ladies Auxiliary. A shout out to one of our sponsors, The Hitchin' Post, our local tack shop. Be sure and check out their table under the big umbrella, maybe get yourself a nice shirt or hat. And don't forget the beer garden tonight, folks. There's gonna be live music featuring an up-and-coming young singer, Alberta's own K. D. Lang. That's a li'l gal with a big voice. Watch for this..."

Whatever else the announcer has to say is muffled as Lindy sees Nick coming towards her and scurries down to take his hand. In the midst of horses and barrel racers milling around getting ready for their event he draws her into a hug. She feels a rush of emotion she can't name and squeezes him as tight as he's squeezing her.

CAM LARSEN WATCHES his daughter and Painless from across the lot, scowling as he packs up his gear.

"I know what yer thinkin'," Porky says, "don't do it."

"Don't do what?"

"Don't go over there 'n' start somethin'."

"I ain't gonna start nuthin'. Just figure he'd like to know I'm three 'n' a half points ahead of him."

"He don't need remindin' 'n' yer just bein' an ass."

"Hell, you know what a cocky bastard he is 'n' here now, he ain't even gonna git day money."

"He knows it, fer chrissake," Porky scowls. "You'll look like a fool if you go braggin' about it 'n' he beats you tomorrow."

"How's he gonna make up three and a half points? And I don't need you tellin' me what I should er shouldn't do. *Momma.*"

"Looks like you do need someone to tell you. You damn well know the only reason his score ain't higher today is 'cause he drew a damn poor bull. He made a good ride on a poor bull. Could git a good one tomorrow 'n' you could make friends with the dirt. Even if you ride yer bull, three 'n a half points ain't impossible to make up 'n' you know it. What if the scores are reversed? Save yer braggin' until the dust settles tomorrow. Or save yer braggin' altogether. It don't make you look good, it just makes you look like a prick, 'n' you don't want to look like a prick in front of the daughter you finally met."

"You goddamn well know he'd be rubbin' my nose in it if it was the other way around."

"Ay-yuh, but that was before. You really think he'd do it in front of Lindy? To her father?"

"Goddamn yeah, he would."

"Well, then, you just go on over there 'n' make an ass of yerself. I ain't stickin' around to watch." Porky turns and starts to walk away, then turns back and says, "But I wisht that just this once you'd be the bigger man, buddy."

"*Pfft.*" Cam blows out a breath, emits a sound like a feral cat growl and shakes his head. But he gathers his things and falls in beside Porky, taking only one backward glance to confirm Lindy and Nick are still hanging onto each other, oblivious to all the activity around them.

They walk in silence the rest of the way to Porky's camper. Cam drops into one of the chairs in the shade. Porky goes inside and comes back out with cold beers, hands one to Cam, and sinks into the second chair.

Cam twists the lid off his beer, drinks deep, burps, then leans forward elbows on thighs as he picks away at the label on his bottle. After a few moments, he says, "You realize, Stu, my bull was a beige spinner?"

"Ay-yuh, I realize that. Big bugger, too."

"And I rode him?"

"Ay-yuh, I know that too."

"I believe I put the beige spinner curse behind me today."

"WHAT IF THEY DON'T let me in?" Lindy whispers. She and Nick are in line at the entrance to the beer garden. Inside the roped-off area, Melon, Wiggles and Gorgeous already have big red Solo cups of beer and are seated at a table with several other rodeo people. The ticket taker winks at Lindy, rips their tickets in half and reminds them to keep the stubs for a draw later.

"I told you it'd be okay," Nick says.

"I think he knows."

"Sure, he does, but you look old enough. The cops ain't gonna come in here 'n' pick you outta the crowd. Probably won't come at all. But if they do, just dive under the table. You won't have to be under there all that long. You can massage my legs or anything else you find to interest you down there while yer waitin'."

"What?"

"Kidding. Relax. It'll be fine."

They go to where their friends are seated, and Nick introduces Lindy to everyone. Some of the cowboys have wives or girlfriends with them. Lindy is the only newcomer to the group; they're all horse people and of course most of the talk is about horses or today's events or who got what kind of new trailer. One has a daughter her age and they compare notes about high schools. If Nick seems subdued, she puts it down to his disappointing ride.

After the burger, chili and corn on the cob meal that comes with the ticket, the band starts up. The singer takes the stage. She looks to be wearing a skirt that might have been made out of drapes, and hardly appears old enough to be out of high school. A titter runs through the crowd. Then she starts belting out *The Lovesick Blues* in her big voice. There's a wave of applause and the cleared area fills with dancers. The first song segues into a run of Patsy Cline standards before she starts into more current hits like *Rhinestone Cowboy* and everyone shouts along with *Thank God I'm a Country Boy*.

Lindy's never done anything other than disco dancing and that only at teen dances at the Peppermint Stick. She knows how to do the bump and the hustle but doesn't know how to dance to country music. Nick proves to be a gifted two-stepper and when it seems like everyone in the place jumps up to dance in what he explains is a line dance, she's an enthusiastic participant, singing out, "Do a little dance... Make a little love... Get down tonight!" Then there's another two-step. When K.D. starts into *Crazy* and Nick pulls her into his arms for a slow dance, she's ready for a break.

"Wow," she tells him, "I thought I was in shape but you're unstoppable."

"I like your shape," he whispers in her ear. They're pressed together, barely moving. When the song ends and another raucous cowboy polka starts, he takes her hand and says, "I know it's early but let's get outta here. Okay?"

Lindy nods and they leave hand in hand. They walk through the barn to check the horses, then go to the camper. It's full dark now and there's no moon; once they're away from the overhead lighting the sky is ablaze with stars.

"Do you want coffee, um, er, anything?" Lindy asks. She was expecting a make-out session and is surprised when he goes to sit up on the picnic table, feet on the seat.

"Naw. Just come 'n' sit by me fer a bit. I'd love a hug."

She slides over and tucks herself in under his arm.

"I had a wonderful time tonight," she says. "Thank you."

"Yer welcome." He nuzzles her ear for a moment, then just sits quietly. After a bit, he says, "I wish we'd've heard something by now about how Monty's doin'."

"That was awful. It made the rest of the rides really hard to watch. Especially yours, coming right after..."

"They should've sent the paramedics in. Goddamn! We shouldn't've drug him out like that. He swore he was okay. He didn't complain about nuthin' 'n' he sat up okay. I thought he just had his bell rung. I should've known better." Nick takes several deep breaths, clears his throat, wipes his face on his sleeve. Then in a husky whisper, says, "Just before he collapsed, he said he couldn't feel his legs."

"Oh my god!"

"Yeah. I might've made him a paraplegic by movin' him like that." A spasm courses through Nick's body; Lindy realizes it was a sob, and that he's struggling to keep from crying. "He's lyin' in a hospital bed not knowin' if he'll walk again 'n' there's me, out drinkin' 'n' dancin' with a beautiful girl like I don't have a care in the world. I must be the worst person on earth."

"Oh, no, don't think like that!" Lindy kisses his neck. "It's not your fault. You're a dentist, not a doctor, you couldn't know..."

"I could know. I should know. First two years of university's the same for doctors and dentists. I have more medical training than a paramedic. I should of known better."

They sit in the dark, not speaking. Lindy feels a swell of emotion. How awful it must feel to think you're responsible for something so terrible. Her heart goes out to him; she casts around for something to say to help him feel better but can't find the words. Maybe there are none.

Finally, Nick says, "I'm gonna turn in early, Princess. I'll walk you back so you can join the others. Give the other guys a chance to dance with you. Take the ticket stubs. Maybe you'll win a draw prize."

She shakes her head. "No. I'll stay with you."

"No, Lindy. I..."

"I want to stay with you." She pulls away from him and gets to her feet; taking his hand, she faces him. Pushing her inhibitions aside, she says, "I want to be with you."

He slides to the ground and pulls her to him; his voice husky, he says, "You mean..."

She answers with a kiss.

WHEN SHE COMES AWAKE in the morning, Lindy remembers she's in the upper bunk, and memories of the previous night's lovemaking come flooding back. The bunk's a mess, sheets untucked, blankets in disarray. Nick is nowhere to be found but his scent is on the pillow with her. She pulls it into a hug.

The camper door opens and Nick climbs in, a large Styrofoam cup in each hand. He puts them down on the table and pulls the door shut, then takes the two steps to stand beside the bunk and look at her. She smiles.

"Good morning, beautiful," he says, and leans in to kiss her. "You okay?"

"Better than okay." She sits up and pulls the blankets around her. He hands her one of the cups; she takes a sip, then looks him over. He looks to be showered, shaved and in clean clothes. "How long have you been up?"

"Little while. Often can't sleep on rodeo days once the sky starts to lighten up."

"Ahh. Nerves?"

"Nerves. Although I sure feel a whole helluva a lot better this mornin' than I did last night. I mean, the *early* part of last night."

They kiss. Lindy's coffee cup tilts and a few drops fall on her thigh. "Oops." she says, breaking away. "That's actually still hot. Anyway, I, umm, really have to go to the washroom."

"Okay," Nick says. "You go ahead."

"Can you, umm..."

"Yer not shy 'bout me seein' you naked, now, are you?"

"Actually, yes."

He smiles and shakes his head. "Oh, sweet girl, we got so much to learn about each other. I guess it'll take some time for you to git comfortable bein' naked with me." He steps away, puts his coffee down, roots through an overhead bin and pulls out a towel. "Here," he says, dropping it on the table and picking his coffee up again. "Go get showered and maybe put on that pretty new shirt. I'll see you back here, or do you want to meet me over at the pancake breakfast?"

"I'm meeting Dad and Porky for breakfast. I wish the two of you weren't so, er, well, I wish we could all be friends so we could eat together."

"Porky maybe, but yer dad? Don't hold yer breath waitin' fer that."

"But you could try."

"I will try. See if you can git him to try, too."

"I will. Anyway, until we're all friends, I'll catch up with you after breakfast. Maybe over at the draw."

"Sure."

"And, umm, Nick?"

"Uh-huh?"

"Sorry about, umm, you know, *this* ..." she indicates the bloody smears on the sheet. "Maybe there's a laundromat in town?"

"What? Wash it? Hell no. I got other sheets. I'm gonna make a flag outta this one, maybe fly it from the antenna of my truck."

Lindy feels her brow pucker and the corners of her mouth turn down.

He takes her cup from her and sets it on the table next to the towel so he can pull her, blanket and all, into his arms. He looks deep into her eyes and says in a soft, husky voice, "I'm kidding. I would never advertise what happens between you 'n' me. You were wonderful. You *are* wonderful. It was a fine gift, Princess, an amazing gift, and I thank you with all my heart."

ELEVEN

Bull Riding – Second Go-Round

High Prairie, Alberta

Sunday July 25, 1976

J ust as the volunteers are clearing away the remains of the pancake breakfast, the skies cloud over. By the time everyone congregates for the draw, rain is pelting down. The tables for the beer garden where volunteers were busy setting up for the afternoon are hurriedly covered with tarps and everyone is herded into the show office. Since it's standing room only, those who need to be there are the only ones allowed in.

Lindy goes back to the camper to wait. She's sitting at the table with a coffee and *Carrie* open in front of her when Nick bursts in, dripping wet.

"Good news, Princess," he says. "Monty has a spinal contusion."

"Spinal contusion? That's good news? Any injury to the spinal cord sounds bad."

"It's not the spinal cord, just the spine. So it's a bruise, a swelling that puts pressure on, well, if not the spinal cord itself, some of the nerves, where they lead out from between vertebrae. Bad enough I guess, but it means when the swelling goes down, it'll heal. Dunno how long it'll take, they say it can be a few days or a few weeks. And it likely happened when he hit the fence, the impact with the fence. Took a few minutes for the swelling to come up enough to impinge on the nerve. Nothing I did."

"Oh, thank god."

"Yeah, thank god." He slides onto the bench seat beside her and draws her into an embrace, kissing her and nuzzling her ear. In a few moments, he whispers, "It's a pity you can't git yer virginity back."

Lindy feels the blood rushing to her face, then chuckles uneasily and says, "Well, maybe I can. I just need rubber and red ink and glue."

"What?"

"It's an old joke, maybe part of a limerick. It's the only part I can remember. Well, I thought it was funny, anyway."

"Oh. Sure, it's funny I guess. And I'm willing to have more stains on the sheets if you wanna go that route. Or do I have to nearly cripple another guy or do something else just as awful 'n' then cry about how sorry I am first?"

"Er, what?" She pulls away from him slightly and sees his pinched expression. The cocky clown isn't in evidence now. "You're serious? You think I only slept with you because I felt sorry for you?"

"It crossed my mind." He releases her and slides out from behind the table to stand next to the door, leaning back against the frame, hands in pockets. He looks at her and then at the floor, then back at her and says, "I'm sorry, Lindy, I'm a scumbag fer lettin' you do it, you know, after we talked about it just the day before. You deserve better."

"Oh." Lindy takes a few deep breaths, then gets up to go to him. When he doesn't open his arms to her, she pulls his hands out of his pockets and holds them. "I wasn't feeling sorry for you. It was just—I don't know, exactly. Well, I did think it must be awful to feel responsible, and I guess I felt sorry about that, but it was more because for the first time, you were *real.*" She rises onto tippy toes and gives him a quick kiss. "You are sexy, the sexiest guy I've ever known, but until that moment, it seemed like that was all there was to you. Then suddenly, there you were, a beautiful human being."

"Oh. Yeah?"

"Yeah. And anyway, what's going on? What brought this on now? I thought we were good, all good, before breakfast."

"I don't know, Princess. I was thinkin' 'bout this since last night, really; it was in the back of my mind that I was taking advantage of yer kind heart even when I was loving you, but I did it anyway. Like minutes before, I thought I was the worst person in the world, 'n' then I sank even lower. This morning a weight lifted off me when I heard the good news about Monty, but there was still this other thing niggling at me. I guess I just had to apologize. Try 'n' square things with you. It would take a load off my shoulders if you could forgive me."

"Forgive you? That's easy, I forgive you." He looks skeptical so she adds, "It's not like there was nothing in it for me, you know."

"Oh. It was okay?"

"Better than I expected." She kisses him again. Embarrassed, she drops her forehead to his shoulder, pushes her inhibitions aside for the second time in two days, and whispers, "I've been thinking about it. I can't wait until next time."

His arms go around her and he pulls her in close. "Jesus, Lindy. Do you know what you do to me?"

He frog-marches her back the four steps to the bunk then hoists her up onto it and starts undoing the snaps on her shirt. He reaches around her to unhook her bra as he scuffs away at his boots; once they're off, he scrambles up beside her.

"Oh. Now? Is there time?"

"I don't want to give you time to change yer mind. You don't care about the team roping, do you? I'm not needed for about an hour. I could probably be done here in a minute if you tickled me a little so hold off 'n' I'll try and make it worthwhile fer you, too."

NICK IS SCRAMBLING to get dressed while Lindy stretches, enjoying the afterglow, then rolls onto her side to watch him buckle his belt and pull on his boots.

"Oh, by the way, Nick. You didn't say which bull you drew today."

"Didn't I?

He's looking away from her, and something in the set of his jaw and the stiffness in his shoulders makes her wonder why he's being so uncharacteristically evasive. What is he not telling her? She gathers her shirt around her and sits up. "What is it, Nick? Which bull did you draw?"

"Well, um, Diablo."

Lindy sucks in a sharp breath and feels a blanket of cold fear settle over her.

Diablo is the bull that nearly crippled his rider the day before.

THE RAIN LASTS AN HOUR or so, and then skies clear and the sun comes out hard and hot, sending up clouds of steam from blacktop and dirt alike. More than enough to settle the dust, it makes the infield muddy in places but otherwise dries fairly well.

By the time Nick and Lindy make an appearance at the in-gate riding double on Petey, the team roping is over and the big steers are being run in for the steer wrestling. Gorgeous is sitting on his horse craning his neck around. The frown leaves his face when he sees Nick.

"Sorry I'm late, buddy," Nick says. "Ran into a little scheduling conflict." He gives Lindy's hand a squeeze and she slides off Petey's rump to the ground.

Gorgeous gives Nick an odd look, then he appears to have a Eureka moment, and breaks into a grin. Lindy feels herself blushing.

Gorgeous is the only one of their group who is a steer wrestler, one event where his size is a definite asset; Nick is his hazer, and Lindy chuckles when she sees sweet-tempered little Petey pin his ears and push the steer over so Gorgeous can drop onto him perfectly. His time is 5.3, faster than Saturday, not enough for the combined score win, but still good enough for day money.

Nick wins the calf roping, only because Diamond is a little excited; Cam misjudges his eagerness and is too quick out of the box, breaking the barrier. If not for the ten-second penalty, Cam would have won by a tenth of a second.

Cam takes top honors in saddle bronc on a big black horse called Jester, which Lindy says must have been meant for Nick, but Nick doesn't do saddle broncs, and of course Jester isn't in the bareback pool. He has to settle for a horse called Miss Kitty.

Miss Kitty bucks well, but Nick gets off balance when she hinks left, away from his hand, and he never really gets his rhythm back. He places third, still in the money, but the difference in winnings between Cam's first place saddle bronc ride and Nick's third in bareback is considerable and in the standings for the year, that's what counts.

As entertaining as all the events are, Lindy can't stop obsessing over the bull riding and it's never far from front of mind. Much too soon, it's less than an hour away, the first event after the lunch break. It's a crowd-pleaser and the stands are already starting to fill, when the four cowboys and Lindy gather around the picnic table. She sits quietly, listening as the men dissect their rides.

Painless points out how unlucky it was that Cam's horse leaped ahead so fast he broke the barrier and got the ten-second penalty when he otherwise had a winning time in the calf roping.

"He's gittin long in the tooth 'n' he's lame half the time," Melon says. "I wouldn't of thought he could move so quick."

"I wouldn't of thought the horse could, neither," Painless says, and everyone laughs.

Then the talk turns to the bulls, and Lindy's brain treats her to instant replays of the big brown bull smashing Monty into the stanchion over and over again as if on a continuous loop. She tries, but can't stop it, and a cold bolus of fear settles in the pit of her stomach. She can't share her concern with Nick; he doesn't need that added to whatever he's doing to mentally prepare, and she's worried her face reflects how sick she's feeling.

Almost unnoticed, she slips away from the group and goes into the camper where she stretches out on the bunk. She squeezes her eyes shut and buries her face in a pillow, imagining awful possibilities, dreading having to watch Nick get on that crazy bull.

She left the group to escape the rodeo talk, but the men's voices drift in through the open window at her head. She's about to close it to shut out the conversation, when she hears her father's voice.

"Good afternoon, ladies."

CAM WHISTLES AS HE runs a brush over Diamond's withers. The barn is a hive of activity with the beautiful girls of barrel racing buzzing around everywhere, getting tacked up. He enjoys their banter, makes a few suggestive remarks that set them giggling, exhilarated when they appear as interested in him as he is in them.

He knows a lot of them, of course, but there's one newcomer on the tour he'd like to get to know a lot better. She might not be much over twenty, but she's been giving him looks that tell him she's no rookie in one department at least. He gives her a wink as he walks past her on his way out of the barn and feels a surge of sexual excitement when she locks eyes with him and smiles. Nothing like being a winner to attract the ladies.

There's some prime gals in Helena, too, though, he thinks. The Americans are less inhibited than Canadian girls. Saves a lot of time, not so much hanging around buying them drinks and chit-chatting.

He wonders about those two young ladies he got to know a few years back that were happy to get poked even standing up. That threesome in the ladies can on his last night in town was something else. They were young enough they might still be around. Damn that rigged poker game that left him without the wherewithal to travel that far, not to mention owing the goddamn rip-off farrier for the shoes Diamond didn't need in the first place.

If he'd gone to Helena, with its much bigger purse, he'd have won more money. But then, he might have won nothing at all. He's already won more at this rodeo than at Ponoka, which is on par with Helena, but day money when you finish fifth is barely worth talking about, even at the Calgary Stampede. And he got skunked there. Why? Stiffer competition? Better rough stock? He doesn't think so. He might've at least got day money in steer wrestling, but Diamond was never good in mud, slipped, and fell. Didn't bother with it at this show because of goddamn Porky. Lousy hazer. He should see if he can get someone else. Or just give it up. It's his least favourite event anyway.

He was lucky to be invited to Calgary even if it was only for three events. You only need two for the all-around title, but it's nice to have some to fall back on, in case shit happens, like Diamond falling. Might not get invited back if his luck doesn't improve, though. Turning out of the semi-final might not make the committee happy with him either, even though he got the doctor to write a report about his swollen wrist.

Things are on the uptick now, though. A week of ice on his wrist and the swelling's gone down, hardly painful any more. His scores yesterday and today are good enough to put him in the money anywhere. Aside from the little glitch breaking the barrier in calf roping, it seems his luck has turned, and this little open rodeo at High Prairie has been the turning point. So it's good he came here.

Besides, if he'd gone to Helena, he wouldn't have met his daughter. Well, he wouldn't have met her this week-end, that is. Likely would've sooner or later, since she was following the rodeos looking for him, so it really wouldn't have been a loss. She must be some scrappy determined little girl, coming after him like she did.

It's a thorn in his side, her being with that cocksucker Painless, though. If he hadn't met Lindy for a month or so, maybe she'd have dumped him by then and he wouldn't have had to see it. The two of them can't last long, not the way Painless is with the girls. Now that he's beaten Painless in a couple of events and nearly beaten him in others, it would be sweet to rag on him about his daughter dumping him too. He savors that thought and it comes to him that sweet moment will happen soon enough, so it's something to look forward to. Goddamn Porky won't have anything to say about rubbing Painless' s nose in it once Lindy is out of the picture.

He walks out the end doors and follows the shade around the side of the barn heading for his camper, when he sees Painless and his friends. They're clustered around the picnic table, yimmer-yammering with everyone who stops by on their way to where ever, probably congratulating them on how great they've been doing and wishing them luck. No one has wished him luck, and he could use it, what with Diamond falling in Calgary, and getting the speeding ticket this morning. Painless would have been beat if not for that speeding ticket, but do you think he'll remind anyone? Not likely.

So there the five of them sit. Painless and Lindy have their backs to him; he reaches around her and gives her a squeeze, then says something that makes them all laugh. Melon looks his way and acknowledges him with the lift of his chin. Cam ignores them and makes a beeline for his camper, where he digs out a bottle of rye, spins the lid off, and takes a few good swallows. It burns all the way down before the pleasant warmth starts. He promises himself that with his winnings he'll buy better booze. He's on a roll now. No more of this rotgut. Nothing but Crown Royal from now on.

Porky went to the shitter and then he was going to get a hamburger. Said he'd meet up with Cam at the concession. As if he doesn't know that Cam would barf his guts out if he tried to put a grease burger in his stomach before a ride. Amazing how Porky can always eat, even on rodeo days. For Cam, it's coffee for breakfast, rye for lunch. More than that and his stomach rebels. Docs told him he has ulcers and should knock off the booze. What do they know? His old man had ulcers too. It just runs in his family.

He takes a few more swallows of rye, another swig to wash down half a dozen Aspirins, then he pops a couple sticks of Doublemint into his mouth and gives them a good chew before stepping back outside. He lights a smoke and thinks he'd better head for the shitter before he has to go to the chutes, too, when he looks across the lot and notices Lindy is no longer sitting with Painless.

No Porky in sight. No Lindy hanging on Painless. This is an opportunity he can't pass up.

He takes another drag on his cigarette, then crushes it under his boot and strides over to Painless and his three shithead friends. Their conversation stops when he holds up at the head of their table.

"Good afternoon, ladies," he says, giving them a wide smile.

"Hey, Gobbler," Melon says, "what's up?"

"Oh, I was just wonderin' how Painless is enjoyin' lookin' like such a loser in front of his new girlfriend."

Melon gives a snort and Gorgeous stiffens as if ready to get to his feet.

"Pretty sure yer familiar with that feelin' yerself, ain't you, Gobbler?" Painless replies.

"Well, he probably don't remember," Melon says, "bein' as he ain't been able to git a girlfriend for so long he prob'ly thinks his dick is just fer pissin'."

"Only as long's his right hand's outta commission," Gorgeous says.

"*Anyway*," ever the peacemaker, Wiggles interjects, "that's rodeo. You win some, you lose some."

"Looks like you can't figure it out, Gobbler," Melon continues, "so I'll help you out. Painless is ahead of you in the standings."

"Yeah, I deduced that. He wouldn't be, though, if not fer that speedin' ticket I got, would he?"

"A win's a win," Wiggles says.

"What's yer point?" Painless asks.

"My point is: yer what they call a seven-day wonder in sports. Yer seven days have came to an end 'n' when yer gone, no one's even gonna remember yer name."

"We still got another event this afternoon, Gobbler," Melon reminds him.

"I beat him in the bull ridin' yesterday. I'll beat him this afternoon too. I drew another good bull today, 'n' I'm back, baby."

"I drew a good bull too," Painless tells him.

"Ay-yuh, I know. But them Mexican fightin' bulls ain't fer girls. You know he's been on the tour fer 'bout three years now 'n' he ain't been rode yet, 'n' you sure ain't got a hope in hell of ridin' him. You'll be lucky if he don't kill you. Maybe you should turn out 'n' save yerself a dirt sandwich. Too bad yer too old fer the sheep ridin', but how's Petey at runnin' barrels? Maybe it ain't too late fer you to enter the ladies' barrel racin'." He barks a laugh, turns and strides off, buoyed with the euphoria that comes with putting that smart-ass cocksucker in his place.

"Good luck to you, too," Painless calls after him.

One of the others says something more quietly. Cam thinks he makes out the word "asshole".

He snorts, but otherwise ignores them. As he nears the washrooms, he sees the new barrel racer standing with her horse just outside the warm-up ring, and walks up to her.

"Hey, darlin'," he says, "I bin meanin' to say hello. I'm Cam."

"Hi Cam. I've seen some of your rides," she says. "I'm Darla."

"Pleased to meet you, Darla. Tell me a little somethin' about yerself Darlin' Darla. Yer horse looks good 'n' you got her all polished up nice too. Can she run?"

"She can run. Off the track. Bear Hug breeding."

"Ay-yuh, them Bear Hug horses is bred to run. What was yer time yesterday?" He slips an arm around her shoulders. Darla doesn't push him away.

LINDY STEPS OUT OF the camper just as Melon is saying, "What an asshole," and looks up at her. She fixes a neutral expression on her face and doesn't let on that she heard what he said or realized he was talking about her father.

As much as she doesn't want to think badly of him, her father's words are unsettling and have added to her angst. Her stomach is squeezing so hard it's painful. Why would he say what he did to Nick right before he has get on that dangerous animal? To try and psych out a competitor, put him off his game, even if it means he could be seriously hurt because of it? How is Nick taking it? From the look on his face, he's brushed it off. There's no telling if he's really put it out of his mind or if his calm demeanor is just a façade.

"We should boogie," Wiggles says, getting to his feet. They all stand and head to the chutes. No one is talking. Lindy squeezes Nick's hand and gives him a hug and a kiss before she climbs to the viewing stand and he goes to join the cowboys behind the chutes.

Wiggles and Gorgeous are both ahead of Nick in the order of go today, and both have rides that go about as smoothly as bull rides can go. That is, their bulls aren't crazy in the chute, neither of them gets clocked by a horn or stomped on or kicked, and both bulls make only short, half-hearted charges before heading for the catch pen. Wiggles scores 75.9; Gorgeous gets 77.0 but his bull petered out at the end, barely bucking, so he is awarded a re-ride option. The other cowboys have bad luck, only one rides to the horn but barely, and he scores less than Wiggles.

At last, it's Cam's turn. He drew a small bull known to go high and drop and he does that on his first jump out of the gate. He spins, leaps seemingly from spring-loaded legs straight up, and is so quick Lindy can hardly believe her father stays with him. When the horn blasts and Cam is flung to the ground, the bull turns and comes at him as if to root him with his horns, but the clown smacks him on the nose. The bull spins and lunges toward the clown; Cam gets to his feet and scrambles up the fence before the bull turns back toward him. It's a good ride and he scores 87.5 to go to the top of the day's leader board with a combined score of 172.5.

Nick needs a score of 92.0 or better to win the combined score. Lindy chews at her lower lip, remembering the scores from the day before: Nick's 81.5; her father's amazing ride today that didn't score 90. She wonders if it's even possible to score 92.

And even more puzzling: why was her father the first to mention Diablo is a Mexican fighting bull? Even without knowing that, having seen how fractious Diablo was the day before, she'll settle for Nick just coming out of it alive.

NICK FOCUSES ON GETTING his rope brushed and rosined, trying to force Gobbler's warning out of his mind. Still, it keeps coming back: *You'll be lucky if he don't kill you.*

It doesn't help that Diablo is known to be mean, tried to smash Monty against the chutes, or that he took after everyone in the arena before going into the pen. The scared look Lindy gave him, her reluctance to let go of his hand when they parted, preys on his mind as well.

The chute boss tells him he's up; he tries to concentrate on the details of getting ready to ride but it goes by in a blur. Gorgeous and Melon are on the rails along with the flanker; when Diablo bellows and tries to climb out the front of the chute just as he did yesterday and Nick's left foot slips off the rails, they have him up and out of harm's way. The bull settles and he's on him again, rubbing his rope, laying it over his hand, pounding his fingers down. He sits back and takes several deep breaths. His feet are up on the bull's shoulders. He nods. The gate swings open. The bull leaps into action. Nick jabs his spur hard into his right shoulder in hopes it will move him away from the chutes and he twigs to the notion it seemed to work. Then he's riding a leaping, kicking tornado and his unconscious mind takes over.

He's about to be launched when he hears the horn. Diablo throws in a leaping twist and he's bucked off into the well in the middle of a spinning whirlwind. The bull is spinning away from his hand and he can't get loose. Another jump and he manages to free it but not before the bull swings his head around, hooks him with a horn, and throws him over his back. He lands flat. Scrambles to his feet. Diablo charges and smashes into his chest. He's knocked down but before the *OHHH!* from the crowd even settles and before the bull can grind him into the ground, the clowns are all around him and distract him.

The mounted cowboy gets a rope around his horns and his little Quarter Horse pulls him a few steps away before Diablo bellows and lunges at him. He charges the horse for only a heartbeat then spins away, seems to look for something that can't move as fast and sets his sights on Nick, who's still on all fours. When he charges back toward Nick and the clowns, the pick-up rider gives one last pull, and loses the lasso. The horse, only half the bull's weight, couldn't stop him from charging and might get hurt if he tried, but they'd created enough of a distraction for Nick to scramble the last few feet to the fence and start to climb. Gorgeous leans over the rails, grabs his belt and hoists him to the top a fraction of a second before Diablo gets there.

After a few more tense moments, Diablo, still wearing the flank strap and dragging the lasso, charges one of the clowns right into the catch pen. Cowboys slam the gate shut behind him and the clown appears on top of it, safe. The crowd's cheer is almost deafening.

"Ladies and Gents, looks like everyone's okay," the announcer cries once the crowd noise has abated, "This bull goes by the name of Diablo. Diablo means Devil and you seen him earn the name here this afternoon. In thirty outings, he's never been rode. Tonight, our own Nick Wilson done it for the first time. And look at that score. 90.0 for the young cowboy from St. Albert."

Now the cheering is even louder.

Nick, down off the chute, holds up both arms in acknowledgement. No one seems to care he has to settle for day money.

No one, maybe, except Cam.

Gorgeous turns down his re-ride. He settles for third place, and day money.

"YER AWFUL GODDAMN PISSY fer someone who just won a bag fulla money 'n' got a date with a pretty girl besides," Porky says. He clears a space and then thumps a bottle of Chivas Regal on the table. "Where's yer clean glasses?"

Cam stops scowling at the overhead bins in his camper where he's been trying to stuff sheets, blankets, clothes and anything else he can in a frantic effort to tidy up. He turns to the pile of dishes on the counter and comes up with a couple of plastic cups, handing one to his friend and holding out the other to be filled. "These clean enough fer you, Mr. Hoity Toity? 'N' I got a right to be pissy," he says.

Porky screws the lid off the scotch and pours two fingers into his friend's glass before doing likewise in his own. They bump cups; Porky says, "Here's shit in yer eye." They both shoot the rye, and refill their glasses.

"Ahhhggh." Cam growls. "Good stuff. That kinda shit I don't mind in my eye. It's the other shit pisses me off."

"Oh, I mighta known you'd find something to be pissed off about. Painless, I imagine?"

"Well you seen him. Loungin' around over there, everyone makin' a big fuss over him, makin' sure he's got ice packs 'n' cold beers 'n' so on just 'cause he's got a few broke ribs. They even got that gal from the TV stickin' a goddamn microphone in his face. You'd think he was a goddamn movie star."

"Yup, just like they done to you when you wasn't so mizzable." Porky goes to the open door and spits a wad of snoose into the dust.

"And Lindy," Cam says with a snort, ignoring Porky's words. "She comes by here 'n' spends two minutes congratulatin' me before she's off hangin' on him again. Two minutes! Wouldn't even have a drink with me to celebrate."

"I don't have to tell you. Well I guess I do. If you'd make nice with them guys, you'd be over there 'n' we could all celebrate together."

"I ain't got the stomach fer it."

"Then you better git used to it." Porky frowns and shakes his head. "Me, I'm goin' over 'n' gonna have a drink with them. Settin' with you's enough to bring anyone down. I only got about ten minutes before I have to head out 'n' I'm gonna spend it where there's some laughs." He picks up his bottle and screws the lid on.

"Yer headin' out? You ain't staying overnight?"

"Nope. I told you, I talked to Red on the phone. I'm headin' to Whitecourt. She says there's a little pen close out behind the diner and I can put my mare in there overnight. She even got one of her customers to drop off a bale of hay."

"Oh. Makes friends fast, that gal." Cam takes a sip of his Chivas, and slides onto the bench behind the table. "Have a seat, buddy. Let's have one more fer the road, then."

Porky stands quiet for a moment, then shrugs and takes the bench across the table from Cam. "Thought you was in a rush to get set fer yer date."

"I ain't never gonna git this place fixed up in time. Might as well fergit it." He waves a hand to indicate the untidy stack of dishes overflowing the sink, beans and egg yolk with bread crusts stuck in it on some, others smeared with something unidentifiable under the mold. He holds out his glass for a refill and Porky tops up both their glasses. "Anyhow, it ain't just all the fuss they're makin' over Painless that picks my ass you know."

"No?"

"No. You know we had breakfast with Lindy this mornin' and all she would talk about was where did my family come from, do I have brothers and sisters, what was my mother's name, can she git in touch with her, stuff like that. You notice she clammed up real quick when I couldn't tell her nuthin' except my father's name, dunno where he come from 'n' so on. That if it wasn't fer yer family I'd have none. I was just garbage, tossed out like an unwanted puppy. Surprised they didn't just drownd me."

"Well, it done my heart good fer her say since I'm like a brother to you, I'm like an uncle to her. She even calls me Uncle Stu now, you notice? And I'm *damn* glad you didn't whine to her about all that. I know I'm sick of hearin' about it every time you start feelin' sorry fer yerself. Yer dad never fergot about you. He came around once in a while, brought you Christmas presents, 'n' he left you a bunch of land. And don't you *dare* bitch about the way Ma and Pop treated you. They treated you same as me."

"Yeah, they did. And I love 'em fer it. But he didn't have to leave me there."

"Oh, I guess he thought he did. He must not've thought he could take care of you on his own. And somehow you doin' nuthin' about Lindy all these years is better in some way?"

"I never knew—"

"You fergit who yer tryin' to bullshit here? You knew. I told you Marie got in touch with me 'n' you done nuthin' about it fer what, sixteen, seventeen years? And you wonder why she's hostile when you show up outta the blue."

"All right! All right!"

They both sit quietly for a few minutes, listening to the flies buzzing around the dirty dishes, Cam picking at the laminate that's lifting at the edge of the table and avoiding eye contact with Porky. At last he looks up under his brows and says with a sigh, "I guess I should cancel my date. No use even unhitchin' the trailer. Might as well save the price of the steak supper I told Darla I'd take her for. Won't go nowhere. She won't want to climb into my bunk with me once she sees all this."

"Guess you'll have to spring fer a motel room."

"Naww, she's a classy gal; don't think she's even gonna wanna ride in this piece of shit."

"Take her truck, then," Porky says, and lifts his chin to indicate the empty rye bottle and beer cans among the mess on the counter, and more on the floor. "Likely just as well you don't drive, anyhow."

"I can handle my drink, I'm still good to drive. 'N' you know that ain't how it works in our world. The gal drivin' 'n' me in the passenger seat? Get real. Be different if I was some young punk with nuthin' goin' on."

"As opposed to an old fart with nuthin' goin' on?"

Cam fixes a hurt expression on his face and says quietly, "This ain't like you, Stu. What did I do to git you so pissed at me? Or did Red say somethin' against me?"

"Naw, Red never says nuthin' bad about no one, you know that. And you ain't done nuthin' other than just bein' yer old self," Porky gets to his feet with a sigh. He roots in his pocket and pulls out his keys. "Here. Take my truck, just fer tonight. You can catch up with me at the Shell station, you know the one with the diner? In Whitecourt tomorrow."

"Aww, that's awful nice, Stu."

"Don't mention it."

"Say, buddy," Cam continues, "you by any chance got enough loot on you to cash one of my cheques?"

"You know I ain't."

"Then can I borrow a twenty or something?"

Porky sighs again, takes a deep breath, then pulls his wallet out of his hip pocket and digs out some bills.

"Thanks, buddy. Pay you back soon as I git to a bank, tomorrow fer sure."

"Yeah."

"And, umm, I just had a thought. Since you got a pen waitin' fer yer horse, might you take Diamond, too?"

Porky shakes his head slowly and says, "Yeah, might as well. Least then I know he's bein' took care of. Leave yer keys 'n' take what you need fer tonight over to my rig. I'm goin' to git the horses 'n' I'll be back in ten minutes." He goes to the door where he turns and admonishes, "And I mean it, Cam. I want my rig back tomorrow. I wanna head for Medicine Hat Tuesday."

"I hear ya. I'll be at the diner bright 'n' early tomorrow."

"Wish I could believe you," Porky says. He shakes his head again and leaves.

Once the door closes behind his friend, Cam gets to his feet, digs in his pocket and comes out with the wad of bills he got when the chute boss cashed one of his cheques. He adds the money Porky gave him to the roll and stuffs it back in his pocket. He smiles in anticipation of the evening ahead. He'll have dinner with Darla, then he'll take her to the game and let her watch him play, making sure her glass is never empty, then back to the camper to give Porky's nice clean bunk a good workout.

He puts on his hat, roots in his pocket for his keys and tosses them on the table, then picks up his bottle and heads over to Porky's truck, a bounce in his step.

LINDY IS SITTING IN the folding chair next to Nick's in the shade of the trees near the picnic table. She's adjusting the towel that holds the icepack on his wrist in place and looks up when Porky's truck approaches and parks in the row of trucks on the far side of Melon's camper.

"I'll be go to hell," Melon says, "It's Gobbler in Porky's truck. I saw his rig pull out, thought he left. Wonder what he wants."

"See, guys," Lindy says, "I told you he wouldn't leave without saying goodbye to me."

"What's he doin' in Porky's truck, though?" Wiggles wonders.

They watch Cam get out of the driver's seat and go around the back of the truck, where he meets up with his passenger. The two of them approach the picnic table hand in hand.

"Fellas," Cam says, "thought I'd stop by and congratulate you all on makin' such a good showin' this weekend."

Everyone murmurs their thanks but they all remain rooted to their seats, watching Cam through narrowed eyes.

"I want to congratulate Painless especially, first cowboy to ride Diablo. It was a helluva show, Painless. Hope he didn't hurt you too bad."

"Not too bad," Nick says.

Lindy gets up and comes to stand beside her father and says, "Hi. I'm Lindy."

"She's my daughter," Cam tells Darla.

"Pleased to meet you, Lindy," Darla replies. "Your dad had a good rodeo."

"Yes, he sure did."

"Everyone! You might not've met Darla bein' as she's new, but yer gonna see a lot of her. She got third in the cans today," Cam tells them. "Nineteen seconds flat."

"You're a barrel racer?" Lindy says, giving Darla, who hardly looks older than herself, a smile. "That's a good time. Congratulations."

"Thanks. It's not good enough for the big time, but we're workin' on it."

The guys all congratulate Darla, too; then Cam says, "Well, we gotta make tracks. I'm so hungry I could eat my horse. We're headin' fer the steakhouse." He puts an arm around Darla's waist and herds her back toward the truck. He drops his hand to cup her ass for a second, then turns back to the group and asks, "Where you all goin' next?"

"Medicine Hat," Melon replies.

"Oh yeah? Me 'n' Darla too." Cam flashes a movie-star smile. "See you there, then." He turns and continues to walk away with Darla under his arm.

"Bye, Dad!" Lindy calls out.

He lifts his free hand in a casual wave.

As they watch them get into the truck and drive away, Gorgeous shakes his head and says, "What the hell was *that* all about?"

"Oh, I know what it was about," Melon says, "you saw him grab her ass, didn't you?"

Lindy's shoulders slump. Would he even have introduced her if she hadn't gone to stand beside him?

TWELVE

Calgary, Alberta

Labor Day 1976

Lindy is at the kitchen table. She chose the chair at the back so she'd have the table as a sort of fortification, a barrier against Arthur and her mother, both of whom are glaring down on her from the other side.

"I'm not giving you all that money so you can flit around all over the country with a bunch of low-lifes," Arthur assures her. "You go to that university or I'm taking it all back."

"She'll go," Marie says.

"I'll go," Lindy agrees, "just not right now."

"Not right now? When, then? Next year? The year after that?" Arthur demands.

"I don't know. Maybe I'll just take a year off. A lot of kids do that."

How did the summer slide by, as effortlessly as the river? Lindy muses. It seems like it was just a few days at home here and there when Nick and some of the other cowboys flew to rodeos; a week at Nick's; a couple of days at her Dad's; on the road to those rodeos within reasonable driving distance, and summer's gone.

"Sure, and a lot of those kids end up never going," Arthur says, breaking into her reverie.

"What's going to be different next year?" Marie asks. "I agree with Arthur. If you don't go now, you might never go. You've been talking about going to university since you were in grade eight. You should get on that plane on Wednesday."

"I can't explain it. I just can't go now."

"You should cut her off, Dad," Jillian appears in the doorway to the basement wearing a smug grin. "She's never going to go. I knew she wouldn't."

"You enjoy hovering in the stairwell eavesdropping?" Lindy asks her. *I wish I'd stuck a needle through all her condoms when I had the chance*, she thinks, *although she's probably on the pill by now so it wouldn't be the same.*

Marie turns to look at Jillian and draws herself up. "Nobody asked for your two cents worth, Jillian," she says. "This has nothing to do with you."

"Marie!" Arthur snaps, "it's a family matter and it affects all of us."

Lindy is astonished her mother would say anything to put Jillian in her place, but of course Arthur takes Jillian's side, and her mother shrinks back. Lindy boils at the self-satisfied smirk on Jillian's face.

"It's because of that *cowboy*," Jillian says. "She doesn't want to leave that *cowboy*."

"You know, Jillian, you're right. I don't want to leave *that cowboy*, but I will, next year. Right now, it's more about my father. I just met him. I'm just getting to know him. I have this nagging feeling that I need time with him and it has to be now because this might be my only chance. I just can't go now."

"See, Marie? We wouldn't be having this discussion if you hadn't kept that man away from her," Arthur says, and raps on the table. "I'll tell you what. I've already paid for the first semester. If that money is down the tubes, I'm going to defund that annuity as soon as the bank opens tomorrow."

"Oh, but Dad, she's got a *feeling*," Jillian says with a snicker.

Marie gives Jillian a sharp look but otherwise ignores her and says, "He didn't show up until a year ago, remember? Why would I welcome him into our lives then? He would certainly not be a positive influence. In fact, I'll bet he's been telling Lindy not to bother going to university."

"No, he hasn't." Lindy interjects. "I haven't told him yet. And why would he do that?"

"Same reason he ever does anything," Marie says, "for spite." She gets to her feet but then sits down again and goes back to glaring at Arthur. "And you! You're just looking for an excuse to go back on your word, aren't you?"

"I have *never* gone back on my word." Arthur says.

"You can keep your money, Arthur," Lindy says quietly. Despite her anger at her mother over her years of lies about her father, she's pleased to see she's standing up to Arthur. She gives her mother an encouraging smile, then locks eyes with Arthur and says, "I'll get a student loan and still go to university, only it'll be U of A, right here in Calgary, so I can keep on living in your house. I imagine that's not what you had in mind, me staying here, is it? There's a reason you chose Queen's, isn't there?"

Arthur's eyes narrow. He looks off over Lindy's shoulder and says, "I chose Queen's because it's a fine school. Jillian could've gone there too if she'd wanted to, but she, like a lot of gals, doesn't see the point. What is the point, really, when you're just going to quit work when you get married and start a family anyway?"

"Well, not everyone wants to run the French fry station at McDonald's and wait for some man to agree to marry them," Lindy says, looking pointedly at Jillian. Her voice sounds scornful even to her, and she regrets it until she sees the sneer on Jillian's face.

"McDonald's is an up and coming company," Jillian says, "Hal says so. He says there are opportunities for advancement. And anyway, I don't care about that. I'm going to work at Texaco as soon as a position opens up."

Lindy clicks her tongue, thinking about the ass-grabbing Hal DeWitt. She thinks, *really? There hasn't been an opening in that huge company in all the time you've been talking about it? Meanwhile, you have to let him grope you?* She shakes her head.

"We're not talking about Jillian, Lindy," Arthur says, "we're talking about you. And whether you're going to be on the plane to Toronto on Wednesday."

"I'm not."

"Think about it. Think about what you're throwing away."

"I know what I'm throwing away, Arthur, and really, it was very generous of you to offer to pay my tuition. I guess I haven't thanked you. But I can't go now, so if I have to go in order for you to fund that annuity or however you put it, I guess I'm going to have to say thanks, but no thanks." Lindy gets to her feet and sidles out from behind the table. "I'll just get a few things and I'll be going."

She walks past their gaping faces and heads up to her room, closing the door behind her and leaning back against it. Her iron resolve evaporates. Squeezing her eyes shut, she sobs quietly, and wonders, *what have I done? Do I really want to throw my education away? I can still do it, student loans and University of Alberta like I told Arthur, but it means living here for another four years. I know Arthur and Jillian want me out of the house but I thought they'd agree to me taking a year off; I'm younger than most of the kids going into university and I'm spending a lot of time at Nick's anyway. I wasn't truthful when I said staying is mostly about Dad. It's partly about Dad, but Nick! If I go now, what if it's the end of my relationship with him? Why does that thought make me feel so bad?*

There's the chortle of a V-8 engine outside; she takes a few deep breaths, pushes away from the door and goes to the window. Nick's truck is just pulling into the driveway. Gathering the laundry she'd piled on the bed earlier, and pulling a few more blouses out of the closet, she stuffs her duffle bag and exits her room. She makes a stop in the bathroom. When she's done on the toilet, she washes her face to make sure there's no sign of tears, smooths her hair off her face and heads back to the stairs, duffle bag in hand.

When she gets down, she finds them all standing around the entryway. Her mother looks hopeful; Jillian looks like she's got something really awful tasting in her mouth, and grim determination is set on Arthur's face.

"Okay, Lindy," Arthur says as she holds up on the landing, "I came up with a compromise. Since you seem to be determined about this, you don't have to go now. But you can't miss the whole year. Your mother and I agree on that." He turns and nods toward Marie.

"I agree, Lindy," she says, "Too many kids end up putting it off again and again and never going. You've wanted this for years. We, that is, *I* think if you have a little more time to think it through, you'll realize it's a mistake."

"Oh? So, how much more time?"

"You have to start in January. That's another four months, Lindy," her mother replies. "It'll be wintertime anyway, no rodeos then, and you'll have Christmas here. That would be okay, wouldn't it?"

"But if you don't go to Kingston in time for the winter semester and I lose the tuition money I've already paid," Arthur cautions, "that is *absolutely* the end of the money. I mean it."

January. Four more months. Just one semester in Ontario and she'll be back in Alberta for the summer. Time enough to apply for a transfer to the University of Alberta for the rest of her degree. She'll deal with whatever arguments Arthur might have against that when the time comes. If she and Nick are still together, she'll apply to the Edmonton campus. That should satisfy Arthur. And Jillian. It's not a complete win, but as Arthur pointed out, it's a compromise. As much as she thinks she'll be as glad to be away from those two as they will be to have her gone, the angst she felt at the thought of not having the money to go to university surprised her. This compromise is also a reprieve. In four months, it should become clear if her relationship with Nick is going somewhere. If it's worth hanging onto. She hopes it is, but Nick, the jester, is still an unknown. She draws a deep breath and says, "Okay. Thank you."

"You'll do it?" her mother asks.

She nods; they share an awkward hug, and Lindy says, "I will. I'll be at Nick's between rodeos and you can call his mother anytime and leave a message with her if you want. You have the numbers. I'll call to let you know when we're in town, and I'll see you again before Christmas."

She goes out the door and down the steps if not elated, at least satisfied.

THIRTEEN

Brooks, Alberta

Mid October 1976

L indy knocks on the door and sings out, "It's me, Dad," before pulling the camper door open and climbing in.

Cam is seated at the table with a roadmap spread out on the table in front of him; he's busy jotting something down in a small notebook and doesn't look up, but says, "Hi, Baby."

"Hi. Where have you been all day?" she asks as she slides into the bench across the table from him. "Aren't you joining us? A few of us are roasting wieners and Red's got burgers on the hibachi, plus I made a big potato salad this afternoon."

"Really? Potato salad, eh? You can cook?"

"Red's showing me a few things. Mom, well, you wouldn't know, but she's no cook. Hamburger Helper's about the best she can do. I actually cooked for her—made some of Red's recipes—when I visited last week. Arthur was impressed with the pan biscuits. Jillian not so much. Anyway. Are you coming? We're ready to eat, and you have to at least try my salad."

"Save me some. I'll be out in a while." He picks up the half-empty rye bottle and pours two fingers into his glass, then lifts his chin in her direction and asks, "Join me?"

She eyes the bottle in his hand and the empty on the floor. She can't stop herself from sighing as her shoulders slump. "No, thanks," she says quietly.

Cam frowns and says, "Don't start, Lindy."

"I wish you'd come out, join us, before—"

"I said, don't start!"

Lindy winces, folds her hands in her lap and studies them. For awkward moments, neither says anything. Finally, Lindy looks up, notices the lines he's drawn on the road map with yellow highlighter, and asks, "What's all this?"

"Makin' my travel plans."

"Oh? Travel plans? You're going to the States?"

"Yup. All set up. Porky's gonna stay out my place over winter. I'm leavin' Diamond with him. Way easier travellin' with no horse to worry about. Not until after the Nationals, of course."

"But, Dad. Don't you need Diamond? And what about that job at Jackpot?"

"Pffttt. Stay in Rocky Mountain House for the winter? Too damn cold. And I can always borrow a horse if I decide to enter the calf ropin'. Goddamn knee gave out last time I dismounted; I damn near landed on my ass, dunno if I'm gonna keep it up anyhow."

"But... But the job! It sounds perfect. Good pay, even board included."

"Oh, shit, Lindy, it's ain't as perfect as it sounds. I don't mind coachin' the young guys, but they're thin on the ground in January. Maybe that'll change once they git their indoor built, but until then, it'd be mostly the grunt work of lookin' after the stock 'n' so on in forty below weather. That sound perfect to you? Plus, don't you think they'd be pissin' 'n' moanin' every time I took off fer a day or two? I'm not cut out to work fer someone else, least not fer more'n a week or two at a time, 'n' I can do that down where it's warm. And git to rodeos."

"But what if you get hurt down there, so far from home? Why do you have to keep rodeoing?" she interjects. "You've got that land. You could be a rancher, work for yourself. Why can't you just rodeo in the summer like other guys, like Nick does?"

"I'm not like them guys, Baby, you must see that by now. Looks like they're all gonna stick around here. Well, that's up to them 'n' it's good fer you I guess, if yer determined to stay with Nick."

"You know I am."

"And you know I think yer making a big mistake."

"Why? I know you two don't get along but I don't get it. What don't you like about him?"

"He's too old fer you, fer starters."

"There isn't that much of a difference between us, age-wise, really; plus he's young for his age and I'm old for mine. Even Red says so."

"Yeah? It ain't just about *years*. How many guys you slept with? Anywhere near the number of ladies he's entertained in that bunk of his?"

Lindy feels her face flushing and sputters, "Dad, for Pete's sake."

"Yeah, that's what I thought, 'n' that's what I'm talkin' about. Age don't matter. It's about life experience. You ain't got any."

"Well how about me getting life experience with him? I don't want anyone else." She sniffs. "And anyway, you don't really think you can walk into my life now and tell me how I should live it?"

"You think you got a right to tell me how to live mine, though? Jesus, where've I heard this before? Yer turnin' into yer mother."

"I am *not*," Lindy insists. "But Mom's right, about Nick, anyway. I think she likes him."

"She's been snowed by him. Never was good at readin' people. Too trusting. What do you think he's gonna be doin' while yer away at that fancy university? Cryin' on his pillow 'cause he misses you so bad? I don't think so."

"I trust him."

"Well then, that just shows how young 'n' foolish you are. I'm tryin' to save you from heartbreak. Cut yer losses. Have yer fun with him 'n' move on."

Tears well in Lindy's eyes. "How can you say that, Dad?" she sobs. "It's not foolish to love someone!"

"Yer young. You'll git over it."

"I don't want to get over it!" She draws herself up and commands her voice to stop quavering. "But this isn't about him, I don't want to talk about him. I just found you and you're leaving? For months? The first moment we met, you talked about Christmas and how we never had Christmas together and now you're leaving before we could have our first Christmas together? I stayed here instead of going away to university like I was supposed to, to be with you. So we could spend time together."

"Don't put that on me. I never asked you to."

"No. But Dad, why do you have to go risking your life chasing after more silver buckles? That's just... it's really not... it's just *stupid*."

"Now I'm *stupid*?"

"I didn't say *you're* stupid ..."

"I'm on a roll now, ridin' better'n I have in years. I'm makin' my plans 'n' I'm going. Leave it at that." He takes a swig from his drink. "Don't fergit, *sweetheart*, I had a life long before I even knew about you."

"*Sweetheart?*" Lindy jumps to her feet and chokes back a sob.

"Aww, Lindy—"

She spins, takes the two steps to the door and pushes it open, jumps to the ground and slams it behind her hard enough to rattle its jalousie window, cutting off whatever else he's saying. The noise attracts the attention of those gathered around the fire pit. She gives them a little wave and storms across the parking lot to Nick's camper. Once she's out of sight of the group, she presses her forehead against the camper, closes her eyes, and sobs.

NICK LEAVES THE GROUP by the fire and follows Lindy around the side of his camper. He pulls her into a hug and just holds her until she's no longer sobbing. "What's up?" he asks.

"Oh, I'm okay, Nick. I'm mad and frustrated more than sad, really. Would you believe the stupid old fart's not taking that job?"

"Oh." He kisses her forehead before releasing her and taking her hand. "Let's take a walk." Together, they head across the field to the opening in the bushes and onto the path to the river, where they find a convenient rock, and sit.

"So, he's gonna turn down that job at the rodeo school? He say why?"

"Says he won't be stuck in Rocky Mountain House in the winter. Too cold. After the Canadian Nationals, he's going south." She snorts. "They've got rodeos going on all year round down south, hey? I guess he likes being broke. Broke all his life and somehow, he stays alive. Now he has a chance at a steady pay cheque handed to him and instead of taking it, he's just going to keep on living hand to mouth, rodeo to rodeo."

"Well, he ain't exactly broke right now, is he?"

"No, but Nick, he's leaving now? Why can't he at least wait until after Christmas? You know, when I have to leave anyway? Better yet, why not take that job, put down some roots and make a real life for himself?"

Nick picks up a stick and scratches idly in the sand at his feet before saying, "You know, Lindy, he does have a real life. Not what you'd want, but he's livin' the life *he* wants. He's bin doin' great since you came along, made it to the Finals. Hardly more'n a handful of qualifying rides before you came, made it all up since then. You can guess at how much money he's made in the past couple three months, and it's way more'n he'd make workin' fer wages, you know that. And think of it. Pushin' forty, and in the Finals."

"Yeah, old enough to be smarter and he still just wants to be a rodeo bum. How long can he keep doing that? Before this summer, I didn't realize what a dangerous hobby rodeo is. What happens if he gets seriously hurt? What if one of these times he actually gets on a bull as drunk as he gets, thinking it's amusing somehow, or that he isn't really all that drunk, or that he's so damn good he can ride even when he's sloppy drunk? It'd kill him. Or worse."

"Well, any of us kin git hurt. Keep at it long enough and you'll git hurt sooner or later. We all know that. Accept that." He gives her a hug. "Cowboy up! That's what we do. A bull just about goddamn stomped me once. I was on my side in the mud 'n' his hoof kinda skidded off my ass. Hurt like hell. 'N' I had one be-yoo-ti-ful purple, green 'n' blue ass cheek fer a while, I tell you."

"You're all so... So... Goddamn it Nick! You could've been killed."

"Or worse, emasculated. Think about that."

Lindy frowns and shakes her head. "That's not funny."

"It sure ain't."

She leaps to her feet, strides a few yards closer to the river, selects a rock, and skips it across the water. When she turns back, the front of her denim jacket parts and the last of the day's sunlight glints on her huge silver buckle. Her father's 1960 CPRA All Around Cowboy buckle.

"You know, it ain't just a hobby fer everyone like it is fer me," he tells her. "Me, a guy who worked fer us on the ranch was a bronc rider 'n' got me interested. I went in a couple of high school rodeos, rode in some junior events, just happen to have a knack fer it. A couple older guys helped me out 'n' it came pretty easy fer me, so I stuck around. Other guys have to train hard 'n' want it bad. Fer guys like yer dad, it's who they are. It's their life. And he ain't *just* a rodeo bum, as you put it. He's a helluva good rodeo rider. Everyone from Corpus Christie to Chilliwack to Toronto knows his name. Plus there's jobs in rodeo, too, y'know. Hell, he was wrote up in Sports Illustrated when I was still in kindergarten. Cleaned up, he might get work as a color commentator on TV. Short-term jobs. The ones he might actually be able to stick to."

"You're right. He could never hold down a regular job, could he? Wishful thinking on my part, I guess. Can't rely on him to be anywhere on time. And I mean, he's late by hours, not just minutes. I'm surprised he keeps picking up even these temporary jobs."

"Well, they know him. Gobbler 'n' up to six drinks kin still rope, ride about anythin' 'n' is funny as hell. And he can turn on the charm."

"I know. I've seen him in action."

"Well, if that's all you seen, you'd hire him too. But he knows he couldn't stick anything permanent so that's prob'ly why he didn't take the rodeo school job."

"If only he'd quit at six drinks. I've talked to him about A.A. That really pissed him off. He doesn't have a problem, could quit drinking if he wanted to, doesn't want to, period."

Lindy comes back and sits beside Nick again, relaxing into his arms. "Sometimes I think I should've gone home after High Prairie. Then I would've only seen him at his best." She pulls his arms tighter around her. "That's not quite true. I would've had to leave before noon on Sunday."

"Er—what?"

"Yeah." She looks off across the river for a moment before continuing quietly, "I heard what he said to you before you rode Diablo."

"Oh."

"That was a real asshole thing to say. I thought there might be some reason, some excuse for it, that it was a one shot deal. Sometimes things come out of my mouth wrong too and I've done stuff I'm not proud of. But with him, it's almost like he's two different people, a split personality or whatever, and you never know which one you're going to get. What's that old cliché? When he's good, he's very good, but when he's bad he's a complete asshole. But anyway, if I left then, I'd be in Kingston now. And I'd miss this."

"I know it's selfish, but I'm glad you stayed. Damn glad." He kisses her temple. "So, next week end when we're in Calgary fer the Pro Rodeo Canada Series final, you kin see yer momma again. Stay if you want. Or, you kin come up to Edmonton, stay with me. I'd really like you to be with me at the Canadian National Finals in November. Unless a'course you think you kin still git into that university, maybe after reading break this semester?"

She shakes her head. "No, I got that deferment. I have to start in January. I'll come with you, stay at your place until Christmas. If your mom's okay with it."

"She'll have to be. It ain't like we don't have our own space. She doesn't have to keep sticking her head in the door at the crack of dawn if she wants to pretend we're not sleeping together. Time she got the stick outta her ass."

"I'd miss the muffins, though."

"Yeah, me too. Too bad she has to deliver them lookin' down her nose. Lucky she don't trip on something goin' across the yard, not bein' able to watch where she's goin with her nose in the air like that."

"I guess if you grew up in the Fifties, it's hard to get used to the idea of sex before marriage. And there's us, practically living together, right out in the open. Just rankles her I guess."

"Yup, right out in the open, in front of god and everybody so everyone knows we're a couple. Just the way I want it. You think back in the Fifties no one had sex before marriage? They were just sneakier about it. She don't like to be reminded that I was on the way when she got married. I was one helluva big premature baby. I'd move, live somewhere else, but with Dad gone, she needs me on the ranch."

She turns to look him full in the face. "Oh, Nick, I don't want to leave. Maybe I should forget about university. I can type, you know. I can get a job without a university degree."

"Hey, Princess, what's this about? What happened to yer vow not to make the same mistake yer mother did, fallin' fer some sweet-talking rodeo rider and ruinin' yer life? Yer talkin' nonsense. 'Course yer goin'. You gotta think about the future."

"I know. It's just..." Her face falls. "I don't want to think about a future without you."

"Goddammit, who said anything about me not bein' in yer future? I want you with me, of course I want you with me. But I refuse to let you give up yer education. I'll miss you, 'n' I want you to come back to me for readin' break 'n' Easter 'n' summer. And I'm hopin' you can go to U of A in Edmonton or at least Calgary instead of back east next year." He lifts his hat and scratches his head vigorously.

"But..."

"But what?"

"Well, you know," she says, chin down, her voice low, "what if you meet someone else."

"You don't have to worry about that. I ain't gonna meet someone else 'cause fer one thing, I ain't lookin'. Don't worry, Princess, when we're ninety, this time apart won't feel like nuthin'." His voice is soft and gentle; their kiss passionate. They draw apart after a bit.

"Don't ever question how much I want you, Princess. I bin around enough to know. You ain't though. Don't think I ain't shit scared *you'll* find someone else, someone closer to yer own age, with all those single guys in university? Already got yer Daddy bendin' yer ear about how I'm too old fer you."

"You know what I told *him*. Five minutes of being my dad doesn't give him tinkering rights in my life."

"Lucky fer me you are one determined young lady." Nick gives her a grin and squeezes her hand. "But I want you to take some time, make sure it's me you want."

"I know it's you I want. You're not my first boyfriend, you know."

"Well, I'm pretty sure I am."

"I don't mean *that*. You know what I mean. But, it's definitely the pot calling the kettle black," she continues, "I've never seen him with anyone more than half his age."

"He ain't lookin' to marry 'em, though. He can't even have a steady girlfriend, he buggers off with every gal who shakes her, er, every gal who smiles at him, you know that. They know it, too. Fer them, it's buckle bunny braggin' rights."

Lindy nods. "I know. At least now I know why he and Mom split. Ever since I was old enough to think about things like relationships, I've blamed Mom. Now I realize he'd be a terrible boyfriend. It must've been awful for her."

"Well, you know they were together more'n a year. Far as I know he's never been with anyone else that long, fer sure not since I've known him, so it must've been something."

"I guess that makes it a little better, anyway."

They sit quietly enjoying the last of the sun and the peacefulness of the river gurgling by. A clutch of Mallard ducks comes bobbing along, then swims into the cat tails. In moments, they take to the air with a clatter of wings and much honking.

"They should have gone south by now, shouldn't they?" Lindy wonders.

"Well, some stay over winter, I think. There's that open water on the Bow by that factory."

"Oh, right. I've heard about it."

"Some stay and some go. Dunno how they decide."

"Maybe they're too lazy to fly south, or maybe they just don't have the urge to travel," Lindy says with a chuckle.

"Like people," Nick agrees. "You know, I don't really have the urge to travel, least not to rodeos no more. I'm thinkin' I'll quit the show, maybe next year, and dentist full time, year-round. Don't wanna be an associate forever, I wanna git my own clinic.

"Really?" she asks. "Could you really quit the rodeo? When you make such a good living at it?"

"Yeah, the money's been good, fer the past couple years anyway. It's bailed out the ranch, paid down the line of credit. But there's good money in dentistry, too. Takes longer to make it but at least it won't stomp you."

He shrugs and looks off across the water for a moment before turning to her and saying, "Six months ago it was the furthest thing from my mind. I never would've thought I could, or at least not for years. But lately? Well, maybe it's just the time of year, maybe I just need a break, busy summer and all, but when I got on that last bull, I couldn't stop myself thinkin', what if this is the ride where I git hurt bad? Me 'n' Lindy are just gittin' started together, what am I doin' this for? Why don't I git back to doin' the less crazy stuff, just go to a few local rodeos? Or maybe I'll git on the organizing committee, or volunteer as a pick-up rider."

"Clown, more likely," she giggles, knowing that's the most dangerous job in rodeo.

He clicks his tongue and says, "I think I'll stick with bein' a clown outside the arena. I'm not goddamn near nimble enough to jump into a barrel."

"I know. It was a joke, and not a funny one. I really wouldn't want you out there on foot, provoking those angry bulls. It's bad enough watching you scramble to the fence when you're bucked off."

"Hardly even aware of what yer doin', adrenalin's pumpin' big time by then. I guess it's that adrenalin rush that's so addictive. We're all just adrenalin junkies when it comes down to it." He strokes her cheek and studies her face, the little puckering of her brow, knowing as much as she tries not to let him see it, she suffers torment every time he gets on a bull.

Some time ago he realized he was in love with her. He dreads her leaving for university and wants more than their current boyfriend-girlfriend status. Living together or at least her staying with him as much as she does is like a commitment, but it seems too impermanent, too easy to walk away from. For days now, he's been thinking he can't let her go without something more.

He's flooded with emotion. Does she love him too? It's early in their relationship. They've never spoken the words. It's a risk telling her how he feels in case he's reading her wrong. *Cowboy up*, he tells himself, *what's the worst that can happen? She can say no. It would stomp me but it wouldn't kill me.* He takes a couple of deep breaths, and asks, "Think you'd consider getting a business degree instead of law? You could be my business manager."

"What? You mean, for your practice?"

"Yeah. My new clinic."

"Really?"

"Lindy, I'm serious," he says. "I want you to know I'm serious." He gets off the rock and goes down on one knee, taking both her hands. "Lindy Marie Jones, beautiful, sweet, wonderful Lindy. I love you. I want you with me for the rest of my life. Will you marry me?"

She gasps, then nods vigorously and tears up.

"Was that a yes? That was a yes, wasn't it? What's the matter?"

She gives his shoulder a shove. "Nothing's the matter and you know it."

"Oh. Yer happy? You know, some people don't cry when they're happy."

She gives him another shove, harder this time, and he tips backward, but he grabs her arms and pulls her with him onto the ground. Their kisses express the rush of emotion they're both feeling. At last they sit up, then get to their feet.

"Ohhh, Lindy. You've made me so happy. But I ain't got a ring. I wanna git a ring on you before you come to yer senses. We'll shop tomorrow, hit the first jewelry store we come to and pick out one together, okay?"

"Yes, okay. More than okay. But can we tell the others tonight?"

"Abso-fuckin'-lootley."

She snuggles in closer and whispers: "Nick, it's only been a few months, but you know I love you too, right?"

"No, I didn't know, but I believe you do. Good thing too, since we're engaged."

"Well, remember the first time we, you know, had delight?"

"Yeah of course. How could I fergit?"

"Remember I told you I wanted to wait until it meant something? We'd only known each other a week, not even quite a full week, but I was starting to fall in love with you already then. It meant something to me."

"It meant something to me too, Princess. A lot, actually. You had my heart on a string practically from our first day together. Is that sappy?"

"Yes. In the nicest possible way. And because you say sappy things I want to be with you forever, too."

AS NICK AND LLINDY come back into the campground from the path through the bushes, they see Cam standing next to Nick's truck waiting for them.

"Lindy," he says, taking a couple of steps forward as they near him. "I'm sorry, Baby. I was way outta line."

Lindy takes a deep breath, then gives a nod and says, "Fine."

"Oh-oh. Take note, Painless. When a gal says 'fine' like that, you better git ready to suck up big time 'cause it means yer in trouble."

Lindy shakes her head, clucks in disgust and starts to go around him, but he pulls her into a hug and says, "I'm sorry fer that smartass remark too, Baby. I really am. Fergive me?"

"Fine, you're forgiven," she says, but doesn't relax into his hug.

Cam gives her a squeeze before releasing her. "I, er, shit, Lindy, yer right. I'd be a damn fool to leave before you have to go to Kingston. So I'll stick around until then."

Lindy takes a deep breath and studies his face for a moment before asking, "You mean it?"

"I mean it. I think what I'll do is fly down, since I'm leavin' Diamond home anyway. Maybe buy a new truck while I'm down there, work my way back home come spring."

"Oh, Dad, that would be awesome! Christmas together. I'm so glad."

"Me too. And I am sorry, Baby. I just have to learn how to be a dad, I guess. Can you give me some time?"

"Of course I can. And we have time. All the time in the world. We have a lifetime."

FOURTEEN

Calgary, Alberta

July 1983

Lindy is startled by the bedroom door bumping open. Standing in the doorway is Chuck. His thinning forelock falls from its strategic position, and he coaxes it back into place with his palm.

"For Chrissake, Lindy! You're still in your underwear? We're supposed to be there in half an hour. We should be leaving right now."

She pulls a navy and pink paisley silk scarf from the lingerie drawer, slides the drawer shut and drapes the scarf around her shoulders. "I told you," she says, "I've been telling you all week. I'm not going."

"Do you think an invitation for dinner at the boss's house is a request? It's not. And this time, do you think you could be at least talk to a few people?"

"It's just a great big barbeque for everyone in the office. No one will miss me."

"No, it's not for everyone, it's only for a chosen few and I'm not going to let you make me look bad by refusing the invitation." He storms into the closet. Hangers scrape noisily on the rod and in a moment, he reappears with a frilly western shirt. "Can you still get into this?"

She looks at the shirt and is flooded with the memory of buying it at the rodeo in High Prairie the day she and Nick made love for the first time. Her scarf slips from her shoulders and falls about her feet. She makes no move to reach for the shirt being held out to her. Tears fill her eyes.

"Oh, for Chrissake, here come the waterworks. Not this again." Eyes flashing darkly, he flings the shirt on the bed and stomps around the room. "Christ almighty."

"Did you ask about that transfer, Chuck?"

"What? Move away from your mother? Seriously? How would she ever run that crappy store of hers without you?"

"Maybe if we went back to Kingston—"

"I know, I know! Calgary haunts you. Goddamn Stampede haunts you. How many times do we have to go through this? Get over it, for Chrissake." Then softer: "Look. I'm sorry about your father. And your cowboy boyfriend—"

"Fiancé."

"Fiancé then. Why won't you admit it? You barely knew either of them. Accidents happen, plane crashes happen, there are lots of ways to die, and life goes on. I'm doing great here, hence the invitation to the boss's stampede barbeque. I *like* it here."

In barely more than a whisper, she says, "They didn't both have to be on that plane."

"What?"

Lindy looks up, clears her throat and says, "Maybe if I went back to work."

"Go back to work? We're starting a family, remember? You could already be pregnant, did you think of that?" Chuck throws up his hands and looks at the ceiling. "Why didn't I walk on by when I saw you in the campus book store? Beautiful blonde no one could get a date with. The White Queen. White Witch more like it. Sure bewitched me."

Attention back on Lindy, he strides across the floor toward her, his eyes black with intensity. She takes a quick, involuntary step back, bumping against the lingerie chest.

He grabs her, fingers like steel clamps around her biceps. His forelock is dislodged again but he ignores it.

"Always something. Maybe this, maybe that. *Maybe* you could quit obsessing over something that happened years ago, and I wouldn't be competing with a ghost. Or *maybe* you'd rather live at that so-called ranch, that *rat hole* you inherited." He releases her arms.

"But Uncle Stu and Red live there."

"Yeah, don't remind me. Squatters. Don't pay a penny in rent. Could be leased, give us a nice little extra income, but instead those two low-lifes live there for nothing. A very profitable asset that is for us, isn't it? Time we put a stop to that."

"But they pay the property taxes."

"Oh yeah? And how much is that? Precious goddamn little. Great business head you have. A lot of good that business degree I paid for did."

"*You* paid for?"

"We could've used the money from that annuity for something else, something that would do us some good like a smaller mortgage on this place, which would be *goddamn* good, interest rates going up like they have. Not a useless degree you'll never use. So yeah, *I* paid for it. I'm still paying for it."

He steps back and throws up his hands again before putting one on his hip and using the other to jab his finger at her. "You're crazy, you know that. What is it, five? Six years since that crash and you're still going on like this?" He blows out a loud breath and takes another couple of steps away. "You know what? I just realized I honestly don't give a shit. It's your problem. Deal with it." He strides to the door. Turning, he says, "If you're not down in five minutes, I'm going without you. I'll just tell them you're sick. It's the truth, anyway."

Lindy stands staring at him. She knows it's Chuck, but for some reason, she sees Arthur. *My god, I have become my mother,* she thinks.

"*Pfft!*" Chuck hisses and turns away, slamming the bedroom door behind him. His footsteps muffle down the stairs and clatter across the foyer. She hears the garage door opener hum and the throaty V-8 of his Trans Am starting up. It idles in the garage for a bit, then he backs it out onto the driveway and lets it idle there, revving it noisily a few times.

She goes to the window overlooking the driveway and sees he's taken the panels off the T-roof. The sun shining on his head gleams on the bald spot in his thinning hair. He dons the black-rimmed sunglasses he thinks make him look like Don Johnson, leans to his right slightly and then the stereo starts blasting. Tires screech as he backs into the road, chirp again as he blasts away down the street and out onto Southland Drive. He's angry. Again. But for the first time, she's not intimidated.

She returns to the lingerie chest and opens the drawer. Digging through scarves, she pulls out a velvet box and opens it to look again at the tarnishing silver buckles. *Must polish these one of these days,* she thinks, as she runs her fingers across the engraving. She slips the solitaire diamond onto her ring finger, just to the knuckle, clucks, and takes it off again.

She retrieves the worn newspaper clipping she'd hurriedly poked in among the scarves when Chuck had burst in. She folds it carefully along its creases and puts it back in the box with the buckles and the ring, snapping the lid shut. Reverently, she covers it with scarves and closes the drawer.

The satin spread feels cool against her skin as she sinks to the bed. She thinks, *everyone says it takes a year to grieve. Maybe six years* is *too long, but I still think about them and see their faces every day. I try not to cry but I still tear up whenever something reminds me of that summer.*

How can I stop that? I thought being married was the answer, but it's not. Chuck doesn't know me. I haven't let him know me. He's right, there's a ghost between us. It isn't fair to him. He has a right to be upset.

Strange, though. Chuck's mad at me again, and for the first time, I don't care. He thinks it's an insult, suggesting I live on the ranch. He was there once and hated everything about it; I love it there, and he won't go back. He didn't like Red and Uncle Stu either. They look after Diamond and Petey; they're fixing the place up with their own money, and that's worth more than rent. We don't need the money and that place doesn't cost us anything.

For a few minutes, she daydreams about the ranch, the horses, how comfortable it was being with Uncle Stu and Red around the kitchen table. Even washing dishes after dinner because there's no dishwasher is a happy memory. Pleasant smells of Ivory dishwashing liquid and outside, the fresh-mown hay or sun on the horses.

Then she realizes she didn't hear the garage door opener after Chuck left. *I think the assmeat left the garage door open.*

Assmeat? Where did that come from? Funny, it's Red's favourite insult. Why would that word pop into my mind more than half a decade later? Maybe because he called me White Witch? That's the fishing boat where Red got her name. Those first few days with the rodeo people, when she shared that story with me...

She spends a few more moments, eyes closed, remembering so many little things about that week when she got to know Red, and Melon, and Wiggles, and Gorgeous. And of course, Nick. They thought they had years to spend together. The memories are bittersweet.

Months ago, she began wondering if she married Chuck to banish her feelings of loss. He was a take-charge kind of guy; she was floundering and welcomed that. Despite his movie star good looks, the fireworks didn't last long, until now there aren't even sparks and there is little delight in delight. Was it fair to compare Chuck to Nick? Lindy thought it would change. It did. It got worse. For some time now, it's more a chore, not delight. They seldom speak to each other. There's no connection. She has become the toilet.

It's more than just the old grief of Nick's and her father's deaths causing her low feelings. The realization her marriage was a mistake is becoming more and more difficult to push to the back of her mind. Long ago, her father told her to have her fun with Nick; move on; get some life experience. He would've said the same thing about Chuck.

At least her counselor doesn't tout the grief-takes-one-year philosophy. She says everyone's different and grief takes as long as it takes. As for her marriage, she points to a lack of communication as being a big part of the problem and suggests couples counseling. Chuck says he doesn't need counseling. He's not the one with the problem after all.

Staying in Calgary where the Stampede is such a huge event means that every year, the reminders of her father and her beautiful, sweet, goofy fiancé loom large, but Chuck refuses to leave. Maybe he's right to take that stand. Maybe she wouldn't love him if they lived in Kingston, either. Maybe he's remembering how reluctant she was to marry him in the first place. Maybe he realizes what she didn't before now, that she never loved him. Maybe she had only fooled herself into thinking she did. Maybe it's not his fault.

All those maybes.

I'm too young to keep living in this purgatory, she thinks. *No one else can help me. I have to save myself.* For months, the ranch has been beckoning. Tonight, the last night of Stampede, a night fraught with memories and ghosts, the pull is especially strong. In fact, it's irresistible.

She stands, goes down the two flights into the basement to get suitcases, brings them back to the bedroom and fills them with as many of her clothes as she can cram in. Shoes, boots and purses she stuffs in a black plastic garbage bag.

All that done, she gets the velvet box out of the drawer again, wraps in the pink and purple paisley scarf and carefully slips it into the inside pocket of the smaller suitcase along with her birth control pills.

She begins writing a note for Chuck, then realizes here's no point. The only thing she can think of to say is that she never loved him and it's not his fault. The first part is true. The second thing, only partly. It would take too long to explain his part in the failure of the marriage, even if she could find the words, and he'd dismiss them anyway.

She has to use soap and water, but gets her rings off and leaves them in the middle of the kitchen table.

She loads her bags into her Cherokee and backs it out of the garage. She takes the remote for the door opener off the visor and goes back through the garage, hitting the button to close the overhead door as she passes into the house. The remote door opener takes its place on the table beside her rings and the house keys. She goes out the front door and pulls it closed behind her, knowing that when it clicks shut, it's locked, and she has crossed the point of no return.

She stands on the steps for a moment, taking a last long look around the front yard and the neighbourhood, breathing deeply. She straightens and stretches up as if she's inches taller because of the weight lifting off her shoulders. "I'm not travelling light this time," she says to no one, and trots down the steps and out onto the driveway to her Cherokee.

Near Maple Creek, Saskatchewan

July 1983

IT'S ONLY A FOUR-HOUR drive from Calgary to the ranch, but she started late and doesn't want to arrive unannounced at night, so she pulls into the lot at the Holiday Inn in Medicine Hat. In the morning, she makes coffee in the little machine in her room, drinks one cup while she dresses and takes the other in its little Styrofoam cup with her to drink as she drives. She considers stopping somewhere for breakfast, but the delay to do that seems unbearable, the pull of the ranch is that strong.

She drives into the dusty ranch yard before nine. She's greeted by a spotted dog who barks a few times and then stands by her door, tail wagging. She slides out of the driver's seat and gives the dog a scratch behind her ears. Two little boys in their underwear running Tonka trucks in a dirt pile look up.

Red appears in a window, pulling curtains back, her face wearing a puzzled frown. Then, recognition lights her expression; she drops the curtain and in moments comes racing out the door, across the deck, and down the steps to where Lindy stands.

"Stu! Stuart!" she shouts. "Come see who's here."

Lindy and Red encircle each other, Lindy bending to hug the much shorter woman. "Oh, gawd Lindy, it's so good to see you! Come in! Come in! Why didn't you call?"

"Well, it was kind of spur-of-the-moment. Too late, and then too early." She takes Red's arm. "Who are these guys?" she asks.

"Oh, the big one is Charlie, the little one is Johnny. They both got the same middle name, and that's Trouble." She chuckles, her face glowing as she looks at them. She says, "Say hello to Auntie Lindy."

"Hello, Auntie Lindy," they obediently chime, looking away from their road building for less than a heartbeat.

Lindy goes to them, taking each grubby little hand for a shake, and says, "Pleased to meet you."

They give her the once-over with their big, dark brown eyes. "Are you here for your room?" Charlie asks.

"Errr...?"

Just then Stu appears at the door of the shed behind the mobile, wiping his hands on a rag.

"Princess! What a great surprise!" He stuffs the rag in his pocket and bounds across the yard, grabbing her in a bear hug, lifting her off the ground and swinging her around before setting her back on her feet.

She's ushered up the steps onto the deck and Red says, "Coffee's on. You sit here. I'll bring it out."

Lindy sits at the picnic table on the deck as directed. Stu takes a deck chair at the end next to her. Red returns with a carafe and three mugs.

The sun's already so warm that the shade from the rose climbing on the trellis and the umbrella over the table is welcome. The sky is clear turquoise blue except for a few wispy, pink-tinted clouds over the nearby Cypress Hills. Lindy takes in a deep breath, enjoying the smells: roses and whatever the family had for breakfast, and faintly, horses. The only sounds are far-away cattle, birdsong, and rumbling truck noises in little-boy voices. She sighs.

"Wow, you guys. The yard—the whole place—looks terrific. And the trailer. You've really made it homey."

"The deck and porch Stu built last fall really make a difference. But we know we're on borrowed time with the roof. There's only so much you can do with Liquid Rubber. We'd like to build a proper roof over it, maybe next year."

"Workin' on the barn now," Stu puts in. "Gonna be a pretty good-sized wine makin' room in there."

"Yeah, the big galoot's been makin' rhubarb wine. Everyone tells him it's good so naturally he thinks he can sell it."

"Well, we got friggin' acres of rhubarb and even I can only eat so many pies." Stu chuckles and pats his paunch. "Gonna try saskatoon wine next. The ravines're full of saskatoon bushes. Goddamn little ankle biters're gonna hafta learn to pick berries. Time they earned their keep."

"Uncle Stu!"

"Oh, you know I'm kiddin'."

"But they'll hear you." Lindy looks around and realizes they boys have abandoned their dust-raising road building and are on a tire swing out in the grove.

"He loves 'em," Red says. "He shows it and they knows it."

"Tell me about them," Lindy says, topping up her mug before settling back into her chair to continue soaking in the morning.

"Well, they needed a home. We had room. So we applied to foster 'em," Stu explains. "They're brothers, five and three. We've had 'em since Christmas. Applying to adopt 'em. Formal like."

"Lindy," Red grins, "we got married."

"No! Congratulations. When? Why didn't you let me know?"

"Well, we did it in Vegas. We wisht you could've come. But with Chuck, well, we knew we couldn't, so we didn't tell you. Actually, didn't tell no one."

"Sneaky," Porky says as he gives Red's arm a pat.

"We had to be married to be foster parents," Red says. "Even then it was a bitch of a process. Goddamn assmeat social worker thinks we're too old."

"That's in our rear view, honey," Stu says, then turns to Lindy. "You know I wanted to marry her long before that." From the look that passes between him and Red, it's obvious they didn't marry just for the kids.

"Well, I think it's fabulous," Lindy says. "And I've wanted to come so many times. I don't know why I haven't. No excuse for it really, at least since Chuck and I moved back to Calgary. I could kick myself, letting his not wanting to come with me keep me away. At least he finally admitted he'd never come. Been there once, that's enough, he said. He actually refers to this place as 'that rat hole'." She sighs. "How could we see things so differently?"

"Well," Red smiles, "we kinda like this rat hole. I'm glad you realized that vehicle of yers only needs one person in it to git here." They share a laugh. "Now that you know it, you have to come more often. Stay a while. You know, yer room's still waitin' fer you. That's what Charlie meant when he asked if you were here fer yer room."

"Oh my god! You guys." She bites her lip, takes a deep breath.

"Well, we told you from day one you'd always have that room, remember?"

"I guess I do remember, but I sure didn't mean to hold you to it. Especially now, with the boys."

"Naw, it's good fer 'em to share a room," Stu says.

"Yeah, they're learnin' to negotiate," Red adds with a grin, "although sometimes negotiations are of the physical variety."

"Tsk. I'm so sorry..."

"Don't be sorry. It works out."

"Well, okay. If you're sure?"

"We're sure," Stu says.

"Okay. Great." Lindy says. She sips her coffee, then asks, "How about Petey? How's he keeping?"

"Well, he gits thin over winter. Little bugger's real damn fussy 'bout what he'll eat. Diamond a-course always licks the bowl clean but Petey don't like this and don't like that. We started him on sweet feed and that helps. When the new grass comes on, he picks up quick. He's good now." Stu digs in his shirt pocket for something, then shrugs, remembering he gave up the Copenhagen. "Wanna go see him?"

"Stuart Pedersen! I bet she ain't even had breakfast."

"Well, no, but I do, I want to see everything," Lindy assures them.

"Yer tour can wait a few minutes. I'll fix you something." Before Lindy can object, Red jumps to her feet and scurries inside.

When she comes back, she has a plate of still-warm fried potatoes and scrambled eggs along with toast and sets it in front of Lindy, saying, "Sorry, no bacon, but at least there's other leftovers. Not like that summer when we was all on the road. Gorgeous had such a huge appetite..." she stops and sucks in a sharp breath.

Stuart looks off across the yard, then pulls out his handkerchief and honks into it before saying, "You know we got his horse here, too? Looked fer him fer weeks. Found him in a kill pen, imagine that! No horse deserves to be kilt just 'cause his owner was. So looks like we're turnin' into a reg'ler retirement home fer old rodeo horses."

Lindy feels an ache in her throat and concentrates on her plate for a couple of minutes. In that moment, she knows this is where she belongs, with people who are still grieving just as she is and won't put a time limit on it.

After a moment, she gives Red a little smile and says, "Missed your cooking as much as you, Red. These potatoes!"

"Them's our li'l spuds," Stu says. "Sweet, eh? Not just li'l potatoes, they never git big. Different altogether. Thinkin' maybe there's a market fer 'em. So you kin have, like, sweet li'l new potatoes, all year 'round."

"Cowboy, rancher, and now farmer, Uncle Stu?" Lindy teases.

"Dreamer, more like." Red says. "Who's gonna pay fifty cents fer a pound of dinky little potatoes? That's what we'd hafta sell 'em fer."

"Dreams can come true. I got you, didn't I?" Stu grins. "How long kin you stay, Princess?"

"Stu!" Red scolds. "She just got here."

"It's okay," Lindy says. She puts her fork down and pushes her empty plate to the center of the table, then gives each of them an earnest look. "Chuck said something yesterday that really hit home. There's something I want to talk to you about."

After The Dance

I slow the bus and turn into the pick-up lane, pulling to a halt at the curb where there's a queue of raucous, jostling students. As usual, the biggest boys are at the front of the line. Why is getting on the bus first such a big deal? Just so they can get the seats at the back? The smaller kids don't want to be there anyway, so the seats would be theirs even if they were the last to get on. Must be the alpha male thing, like steers butting heads.

I pull the lever and the door opens with a hiss. The boys vault up the stairs, pass me as if I'm not even there, and thunder down the aisle pushing and shoving and squawking. The smaller kids climb on, only slightly more orderly. The teacher follows the last student to the door and says, "Hi, Lindy. John Henry will be a couple more minutes."

"Hi," I respond. "Don't tell me he had to go to the office again."

"Okay, I won't tell you," she chuckles. "But he shouldn't be long."

"Thanks, Marg." I nod and settle back to wait. John Henry had to go to the office again. That kid! What is it this time? And why can't they deal with it during school hours so

185

the rest of the kids don't have to wait? I've got a schedule and would like to keep it. Well, if nothing else, filling in until they find a permanent driver has given me a new appreciation for all that Red had to deal with over the years.

The kids are screaming. Something hits the floor with a thump. A girl squeals, "Get off me!" I get up and stand at the front of the aisle to see what's going on. The offender is immediately obvious. "Terry," I call out, "can't you see that seat's taken?"

"Sorry, Ms. Larsen," he says, and goes back to the empty seat next to his best friend just across the aisle.

"Thank you." Terry is a good kid, seldom any trouble, so this is out of character for him. I suspect he squeezed in on top of the two girls because he likes the one nearest the window, Katie. She must be about eleven now, her little breasts budding, starting to look so grown up. How well I remember being that age, still thinking boys were stupid for doing things like Terry just did, but beginning to like it. Where does the time go?

I get back in the driver's seat just as a white pickup truck pulls to the curb in front of the bus. The driver gets out and comes up beside my window. I slide it open and say, "Hi Jake. What's up?"

"Saw the bus still sittin' here so I thought I'd swing in 'n' say hi," he says, giving me the wide grin that always reminds me of Nick. "Someone late?"

"Yeah. I don't know how Red managed to keep to a schedule. Some of these kids have chores to do at home, and here we sit."

"How's she doin', anyway? Red, I mean. She gonna be back drivin' soon?"

"She's doing okay, not on crutches anymore, but she's decided to give it up. She'd rather be helping out with the wine making. I'm giving it up, too. They got someone hired, but he can't start for a couple weeks. Can't happen too soon for me! Good thing I never had kids. Can't wait for the last one to get off the bus so I can head for my nice quiet house." I click my tongue and look off across the tarmac toward the school, where I spot John Henry strolling toward the bus. "Look at that kid! He's kept us all waiting. You'd think he could hustle, wouldn't you?"

"Ay-yuh. You'd think. But then he wouldn't be such a cool dude." He lifts his ballcap and scratches the back of his head, then smooths his hair and resettles the cap. "I, um, you goin' to the dance over at the community center tomorrow night?"

"Didn't even know there was one."

"No? There was a poster up at the Co-op."

"I guess I missed it."

"Would you though? Go to the dance, I mean? With me?"

"Oh. Umm..."

"Come on, Lindy. Don't say no! I know you don't like the movies but I thought you might like to dance. It wouldn't have to be like a date. Just a couple of friends havin' a good time together. No pressure."

Just then John Henry comes clattering up the steps and I turn to face see the cocky grin on his face. He says, "I know I'm late, Ms. Larsen! Wasn't my fault this time!"

Then he's past me, stirring squawks and hisses from everyone as he goes by. More chaos erupts from the back of the bus. I know without looking that he's trying to bully his way into a seat instead of taking one closer to the front, causing a mass reshuffling. That's John Henry. I sigh, pull the lever to close the door, then turn back to Jake. "Okay. That might be fun."

"Oh yeah?" His eyebrows go up for a second; he stands taller and takes a step closer. Grinning, he says, "Good! I'll pick you up at eight?"

"How about I meet you there?"

"Oh. Sure, I guess. If you'd rather."

"Saves you a bunch of driving. Whoever gets there first saves a table."

"You know I don't mind comin' to git you."

"No, it's all right."

"Okay. If you're sure?"

"I'm sure."

He backs away a couple of steps, shrugs and says, "See you there, then."

"See you there." I give him a smile, slide the window closed, put the bus in gear and steer it away from the curb. When I check the mirrors, I see him standing in the middle of the lane watching the bus leave.

Jake is new in town, noticeable because Maple Creek isn't big, just a couple thousand including the sparsely-populated ranches surrounding it, so newcomers stand out. Stu knows him slightly from his rodeo days and introduced him when we ran into him at the Maple Creek rodeo a few months ago. Jake reminds me of Nick: tall, fair-haired, a rancher and a rodeo rider, too. I'm ambivalent, both put off and drawn to him because of it.

I tell myself I agreed to go to the dance to get to know him better and see if I'm only attracted to him because he reminds me of my first love. It's only one date, and not really a date at that. I don't want to rush into anything. Things went too far too fast with Brett and fell apart just as fast. I won't let that happen again.

I first saw Jake shortly after I started working at the bank. I happened to look up over my typewriter just as he walked through the door, and for a heartbeat, I thought it was Nick. It hit me like a punch in the stomach. I wonder how that's even possible all these years later. Josie happened to look my way and came over to my desk to ask what was wrong. I couldn't tell her. I had to go to the ladies room and I actually had a little cry before I could calm myself enough to get back to work.

All the well-meaning people I've ever known say grief lasts a year, the implication being there's something wrong with me because I still grieve for Nick. Not all the time, of course, and it doesn't always sabotage me like that. It's just that once in a while, it blindsides me. Marriage did nothing to banish it. If anyone was to ask, I'd tell them grief lasts as long as it lasts.

After that, I started noticing Jake around town. At the feed store. At the rodeo. And of course when he comes in to do his banking. I'm not a teller, though, so I'm not at the counter but at a desk in back, and we never actually came face to face. The first words we spoke to each other were when he was coming out of the bank just as I was going back in after lunch. We made eye contact as he held the door for me. I said thank you. He said you're welcome. That's it.

Another day I was at the check-out in the Field's store buying new underwear for the boys when he came up beside me, pack of T-shirts in hand. We paid for our purchases and walked back to our vehicles together, talking about what a cold spring it had been and how late the pastures were greening up. That's right. My first chance to talk to this beautiful man and I wasted it talking about the weather. Such a cliché. But I had just gotten together with Brett; we were still in the can't-keep-our-hands-off-each-other stage, so although I thought Jake was drop-dead gorgeous, I never would have done more than look.

At the rodeo that summer, he came and sat in the bleachers with me. Well, not really with me; with our little group. Stu knew him slightly from back in his rodeo days, and introduced him to everyone. I talked to him a little, just joined in the conversations of the group really, but didn't pay much attention. I was mostly watching Brett, who was all over Diane of the Double D's and that's not the name of her ranch. Poor Diane, she can't get shirts to fit. That snap in the middle of those fun jugs just will not stay closed. Shortly after that, Brett and I split up. In retrospect, it would've been a good time to hook up with Jake and give Brett a dose of his own medicine. Opportunity missed.

Anyway, within a week of Brett and me splitting up, Jake was waiting for me outside the bank and asked me to go to the drive-in with him. That's the thing about small towns, everyone knows everyone else's business. Who's sleeping with who. If you believe the gossip, there's always been wife swapping but in 1985 it's gone wild. Or maybe it's just more out in the open. Seems like it's risky because husbands don't always get their wives back. Maybe that's the point—it's a sensible reshuffling of couples who married the wrong person right out of high school.

I imagine Jake suggested a drive in instead of lunch or dinner because he was anxious to see a re-run of Smoky and the Bandit, or maybe he just wanted to patronize the drive-in so it wouldn't close down like so many have, thanks to Blockbuster, or maybe just because there's isn't much of anything else to do in a small town. But a drive-in movie with a man I barely knew? I tried unsuccessfully not to be offended and of course, declined. Besides, after Brett, I promised myself a year of being on my own.

Some inner part of me must have decided that although it hasn't been a year and in fact has only been a few months, it's time. Meeting Jake at the dance instead of having him pick me up eliminates the possibility of more activity after the dance. A perfect way to make sure things don't go too far, too fast. Sexual revolution be damned.

Author's Note

There was a brief time in my youth when I had a bareback bronc rider boyfriend and entered barrel racing events at small-time rodeos such as Symonds Valley and Okotoks and gymkhanas where ever I could find them. At that time, there were acres of prairie around the show grounds.

My family home was on forty acres near Balzac, which I believe is now under a runway for YYC. The sites may be obliterated and my boyfriend may have run to fat, but in my memory, there is still open range land around Calgary that's hot and dusty and beautiful, and Eddie is still crazy handsome and sexy as hell. The only good thing about moving away is that in my memory, the land isn't marred by subdivisions and the people are, in the words of Bob Dylan, Forever Young.

REVIEWS ARE VERY HELPFUL and very much appreciated.

COVER BY MIBLART

Don't miss out!

Visit the website below and you can sign up to receive emails whenever Gayle Siebert publishes a new book. There's no charge and no obligation.

https://books2read.com/r/B-A-EAZM-ZFCXC

BOOKS 2 READ

Connecting independent readers to independent writers.

Did you love *Silver Buckles*? Then you should read *After The Dance*[1] by Gayle Siebert!

Cattle rustling, dark money and murder in a place where nobody even locks their doors.

When Lindy Larsen's marriage ended, she moved to the ranch in The Badlands she inherited from her father. It has never been profitable so she takes a job in town and plans a farmgate store to put the ranch on a solid financial footing. She gets a promotion and begins a promising romance. The future looks bright.

When some of their cattle are stolen it's a serious financial blow. They miss a payment on their line of credit, tanking chances of getting the loan they need to finance the store. An unexpected source of funding presents itself and the store becomes a reality.

---

1. https://books2read.com/u/mBwgLy

2. https://books2read.com/u/mBwgLy

But the store soon runs into a roadblock and the rustlers haven't gone away, either. Using all-terrain vehicles and semi-trailers, they strike fast and disappear. A rancher who catches them in the act is murdered. Lindy thinks she knows who's behind it. She pokes around hoping to find proof, and uncovers what she thinks is damning evidence. She reports her suspicions to the RCMP, but they can't do much. When her nephew goes missing, she has no choice but to act.

Do the rustlers have her nephew? Can she find him in time? Or will they disappear into the Badlands like so many others, never to be seen again?

"Fans of the Yellowstone tv series will love After The Dance."-Patricia Parker, author of The Abode.

Read more at https://www.gaylesiebert.com.

Also by Gayle Siebert

Lindy Larsen
Silver Buckles
After The Dance
Katawasis Girls
The Bones Below

Lisa Rogney
Call Me Lisa
Wembly

Secrets
The Bear Mountain Secret
The Spirit Bear Secret
Astrid
The Dark River Secret

Standalone
Where The Mule Grazed

The Feeder

Watch for more at https://www.gaylesiebert.com.

About the Author

Gayle has always loved horses, reading, and writing. She has been a trail rider, barrel racer, and dressage rider. Now retired after more than 3 decades as an insurance adjuster, she lives on a horse farm near Nanaimo, British Columbia, Canada, writes, reads, and yes, still rides.

Read more at www.gaylesiebert.com.